Redemption Road

LAUREL VALLEY

LILIANA HART

Also by Liliana Hart

JJ Graves Mystery Series

Dirty Little Secrets

A Dirty Shame

Dirty Rotten Scoundrel

Down and Dirty

Dirty Deeds

Dirty Laundry

Dirty Money

A Dirty Job

Dirty Devil

Playing Dirty

Dirty Martini

Dirty Dozen

Dirty Minds

Dirty Weekend

Dirty Looks

Addison Holmes Mystery Series

Whiskey Rebellion

Whiskey Sour

Whiskey For Breakfast

Whiskey, You're The Devil

Whiskey on the Rocks

Whiskey Tango Foxtrot

Whiskey and Gunpowder

Whiskey Lullaby

The Scarlet Chronicles

Bouncing Betty

Hand Grenade Helen

Front Line Francis

The Harley and Davidson Mystery Series

The Farmer's Slaughter

A Tisket a Casket

I Saw Mommy Killing Santa Claus

Get Your Murder Running

Deceased and Desist

Malice in Wonderland

Tequila Mockingbird

Gone With the Sin

Grime and Punishment

Blazing Rattles

A Salt and Battery

Curl Up and Dye

First Comes Death Then Comes Marriage

Box Set 1

Box Set 2

Box Set 3

The Gravediggers

The Darkest Corner

Gone to Dust

Say No More

Laurel Valley

Tribulation Pass

Redemption Road

Midnight Clear

Look not mournfully into the past.
It comes not back again.
Wisely improve the present. It is thine.
Go forth to meet the shadowy future,
without fear.

~Henry Wadsworth Longfellow

Chapter One

ZOE GREEN STARED AT HERSELF IN THE MIRROR AT the beauty shop and felt the tears well up in her eyes. The haircut wasn't bad. It was just… different.

But different was to be expected. A new life called for something as drastic as a new haircut. Gone were the waist-length white-blond locks that had been her signature style. Along with the hair went the weight of guilt, shame, and embarrassment from being divorced after less than a year of marriage. Everything was lying on the salon floor, waiting to be swept into the dustbin.

The last time she'd had hair this short she'd been four years old and taken a pair of kitchen shears, cutting her curly locks almost to the scalp. It had been her mother who'd shed tears then.

The tears had been followed by a paddling Zoe still remembered. She'd never cut her hair again.

As an adult, Zoe realized if her mother had been paying more attention to her daughter than her personal trainer, then a four-year-old never would have been able to climb up on the counter and gotten a pair of sharp kitchen shears to begin with. But it wasn't often Melody Green put anyone or anything else above herself.

"Wow, you look amazing," said the woman in the chair next to hers. "If I hadn't seen you come in I never would have recognized you. Not everyone can pull off a style that short. And it really makes your eyes and cheekbones pop. It's stunning."

Zoe blinked rapidly so the tears wouldn't fall. She was a new woman, and the new Zoe didn't cry. So she straightened her shoulders and stiffened her upper lip and said, "Thank you. It's definitely going to take some getting used to."

"All good things do," she said kindly. "I'm Raven, by the way. I own the little boutique a couple of doors down."

Raven was an attractive woman around Zoe's age with dark wavy hair parted down the middle and a fringe of bangs that framed big blue eyes. Her hair looked almost exactly the same as it had when she'd come in, only a little shorter, and a few subtle highlights were now mixed in with the curls. She wore big hoop earrings and bright red lipstick. She reminded Zoe of a modern-day gypsy.

"I saw your shop when I got into town last week," Zoe said. "I love the pantsuit in the window."

"That metallic bronze would look amazing on you with the color of your hair and skin. Size four, right? I'll make sure to hold one for you in the back room."

Zoe smiled, deciding the woman wasn't only an insightful salesperson, but she knew the ins and outs of her business well. She could respect and appreciate that.

"I'm Zoe."

"It's nice to meet you. Here on vacation?" Raven asked.

With as much confidence as she could muster Zoe said, "No. I live here now."

"Wow," Raven said, a sympathetic understanding in her eyes that made Zoe feel like she'd just told the woman all her family secrets. "A new town and a new haircut. That's a lot of change in one week."

"Tell me about it," Zoe said. "Not to mention

freshly signed divorce papers, a new book contract, and a new condo." Zoe felt herself starting to hyperventilate and she took a calming breath. No big deal. People made major life-changing decisions every day—maybe not all in *one* day—but it did happen.

As an added boost to her confidence she said, "I'm going to get a dog too."

"Good for you," Raven said, laughing, and then her smile softened. "I'm sorry about the divorce, but it must be exciting to have something new and fresh on the horizon. I'm a big believer in new adventures. They're good for the soul. And if you're looking for a dog, the shelter is close by. Just walk right in front of The Lampstand and then take a right. The shelter is the cute little stone chalet at the end of the block. I'm sure they'll have exactly what you're looking for."

That would be a nice change of pace, Zoe thought wryly—to know exactly what she was looking for. But all she knew was she had to start somewhere. She was alone, but that was nothing new. What mattered was she had her name, her career, and a great view from her condo. Everything else she'd figure out along the way.

Zoe handed her credit card over to the stylist and left her a generous tip, and then she grabbed her Louis Vuitton travel bag that carried her laptop—because she never left home without it—and put her earrings back on. Excitement was coursing through her veins. A new adventure. That's exactly what she needed. Just like the heroines in her books.

There was a reason she wrote novels for a living. Writing had been a means of escape during a childhood with two very self-absorbed parents. She'd been the only eleven-year-old at St. Mary's School for Girls who'd been thrilled at being sent off to boarding school in another state. And then from there she'd gone off to college.

She would have gone just about anywhere to keep from going back to her parents' house where her mother brought one lover after another right under her father's nose. And her father stayed away on business so he could travel with his mistress. Heaven forbid the two of them actually share the same space. That's when the fireworks really started, especially if alcohol was involved.

Writing had saved her. Her first novel had been published before her senior year of college and she'd signed a huge contract to write three more books soon after, so she'd quit college and gone to work full-time writing. It had given her the financial independence she'd needed to live on her own. She'd been twenty-two years old, and she'd only spoken with her parents a handful of times since then. Neither of them seemed to remember they had a daughter, not even on Christmas or her birthday.

Zoe had spent the rest of her twenties making sure she'd never have to go back to that house again, working almost nonstop and accumulating a small fortune in the meantime. And then she'd met Todd by chance while he'd been on a run in Central Park. The sight of him had taken her breath away. He'd been handsome and fit and very charming. And he'd convinced her to marry him in a matter of weeks in a whirlwind romance. And in the span of that year she'd lost her independence and herself. Not to mention a good chunk of what she'd worked for.

Zoe blinked rapidly and shook herself out of the memories. "It was nice to meet you, Raven." She smiled and hoped it reached her eyes.

"Come on down to the boutique when you get a chance," Raven said. "A haircut like that needs a whole new wardrobe."

Zoe laughed. "You can count on it."

"Welcome to Laurel Valley."

Welcome to Laurel Valley. Zoe let the words play around in her mind. There was something about this place that had called to her instantly. Her publisher had sent her to Laurel Valley several years before to do a book signing, and the town had left an impression on her. So much so there'd been pieces of Laurel Valley in every book she'd written since.

The resort town sat like a jewel nestled at the base of white-capped mountains, surrounded by clear lakes and towering pines. The architecture of the town was Bavarian in style and strictly maintained so it looked like a picture-perfect post-card no matter the season. Chalets lined the downtown area, made of stucco or natural stone, and planter boxes streaming with colorful flowers hung from every window.

The downtown area was in the shape of an *X* and at the apex was a two-story building in the same Bavarian style with a pointed black roof and balconies on every side. A large sign that read *The Lampstand* hung over the door and large pots of fuchsia and yellow bougainvillea spilled artfully over the edges.

At the center of the *X* was an area that held wooden picnic tables with red umbrellas during the summer and that became an ice-skating rink in the winter. She remembered the ice-skating rink from when she'd visited before. Winters were cold and long in Laurel Valley.

Zoe noticed the sign hanging under the awning two doors down that said *Raven Layne* and knew she'd be back to the boutique to shop later. For the moment, she felt like she was having an out-of-body experience. Her head was too light, and she had to resist the urge to push her hair back off her shoulders. What did they call it when amputees still felt like their limbs were there? *Phantom limbs*, she thought. Well, she had phantom hair and it was already driving her crazy.

But crazy seemed to be her middle name today because she took a deep breath and cut across the street in front of The Lampstand, and then she took a right toward the dog shelter. She even managed to nod and smile at the people who passed her on the sidewalk. They were most likely tourists here for the summer, and the thought that this was her home now made her straighten her shoulders with pride.

The animal shelter was at the end of the block in a chalet made from the same natural river stone as her condo. Zoe wondered how many people came here on vacation and left with a pet. It seemed an odd place for an animal shelter, but it obviously worked. When she drew closer, she could see why.

Her heart sighed at the sight of a pen full of fluffy puppies wrestling playfully in the grass. A family of four came up beside her, oohing and ahhing, and she could tell by their Laurel Valley T-shirts and backpacks they were on vacation.

"It's our last day here, Phil," the wife said. "We can take one of them back home with us tomorrow. The kids will have the rest of the summer to train him."

Zoe could tell the dad was a goner. There was no way he could resist those three faces looking so imploringly at him. Before she got caught in the puppy trap, Zoe found her resolve and marched through the front door of the shelter.

The last thing she needed was a puppy. Puppies were not conducive to book deadlines. They required lots of playtime and attention, not to mention they required lots of trips outside. The thought of going up and down the elevator every hour and through the night was almost enough to have her run screaming in the opposite direction. But something kept her feet planted to the pine floor of the reception area.

It smelled of antiseptic and lemons, and beneath it was the underlying aroma of animals.

There was a large L-shaped reception desk with a pretty girl behind the counter. She was on the phone, so Zoe walked over to the glass wall where rows of kittens were displayed. There were short-hairs and longhairs, blue eyes and amber, playful and sleeping. They were all adorable, and for just a moment she considered getting a kitten too. They were hard to resist. Which was, she was sure, why they had them displayed at the front of the shelter.

A kitten was not on her list for starting a new life. Todd had a cat, and it had been a miserable, mean, vengeful tabby who'd spent its days looking for ways to sabotage her work and her marriage.

That was probably unfair. A cat couldn't possibly have that much power as to sabotage one's marriage. It only seemed that way because Todd babied that ferocious fur ball more than he had her.

"How can I help you?" a voice said.

Zoe jumped slightly and turned to face the pretty girl who'd been on the phone. She had a kind, round face still softened by youth, a smattering of freckles across the bridge of her nose, and her dark hair was piled artfully on top of her head. She wore jeans and a pale blue T-shirt with the shelter's logo across the front.

"Sorry," Zoe said. "I was lost in thought."

"I figured you must be," she said, grinning. "Most people don't look like they could do murder when they're staring at kittens. Unless they're a psychopath. You're not a psychopath, are you?"

"Not since I last checked," Zoe said. She couldn't help but smile. The girl's good humor and infectious personality wouldn't let her do anything else.

"I'm Mac O'Hara," she said.

"Zoe Green. And I'm here for a dog."

"Oh," Mac said, looking surprised. "Don't get me wrong, but I'm pretty good at matching people with pets. Are you sure you're a dog person?"

"What animal would you match me with?" Zoe asked, intrigued.

Mac stood back and looked her over from head to toe. "You're successful," she said. "Busy life. Busy schedule. And you don't take a lot of time for yourself except for the necessities. Killer hair, by the way. You look like you could fight an army of orcs, be the lead singer for a rock band, and then seduce a Mediterranean prince and sell his secrets to the government."

"That's very specific," Zoe said, lips twitching.

"Are you a writer?"

"I'm a waitress over at The Lampstand most of the time," Mac said, shrugging. "And I work here three days a week. I also go to school, but we're out for the summer."

"Well, you have a very creative imagination," Zoe said. "What are you studying?"

"Business," Mac said. "I don't love it, but I'm supposed to graduate next spring, and I'm pretty sure my dad would kill me if I changed my major at this point."

"That I do understand," Zoe said sympathetically. "Sometimes you just have to keep going and learning so you can discover who you really want to be. And then once you figure it out you can forge your own path."

"Is that what you did?"

"Yeah, pretty much," she said with a sigh.

The chime rang over the door and the family who'd been eyeing the puppies outside stepped in. The father had obviously caved since both children were practically bouncing out of their shoes with excitement.

"Welcome," Mac said, grinning down at the kids. "Talked him into it, did you? I've seen y'all come by a couple times this week to look at the puppies."

"We want the white-and-brown one!" the little boy said. "I'm going to name him Doug because that's my best friend's name, and Doug has a brown spot over his eye just like the puppy."

"I'm sure Doug will be honored," Mac said. "Hold on just a second and I'll have someone come help you with all the paperwork." Then she looked back at Zoe and winked. "Give me just a minute and I'll finish matching you with your perfect animal."

"I can hardly wait," Zoe said, laughing and shaking her head. Whoever Mac O'Hara was, she was a handful.

A few minutes later Mac came back with a man who was wearing the same shirt as Mac. Like all the people in Laurel Valley, he had a summer tan and the physique of someone who spent their off hours on the lake or the ski slopes. He smiled at the family and ushered them over to the counter to fill out paperwork, and Mac waved Zoe to the door she held open that led into the kennel area.

"So how close was I on your personal assessment?" Mac asked her.

"You'd make a fair palm reader at the county fair."

Mac grinned. "Ahh, my ancestors would be

proud. Anything sounds better than sitting in a stuffy office all day for the rest of my life."

"So which one of these is my perfect match?" Zoe asked.

"You're definitely a cat person," Mac answered instantly. "But I have a feeling you're also stubborn and you don't change your mind easily, so I'm open to suggestions."

"You have more wisdom than my ex-husband," Zoe said dryly. "And I'd agree with you. A cat would go much better with my schedule. But I work from home and I have no travel plans for a long while, so I want a dog. I've never had a dog. Dogs are man's best friend, right?"

"Right," Mac said. "Just keep your shoes and handbags out of reach. They look expensive. To a puppy, everything is a chew toy."

"Oh, I don't want a puppy. I want an older dog. One that's already trained and has lived some life. I want a dog with experience."

"Uh-huh," Mac said doubtfully. "I think I've got just the dog for you. And this is his lucky day because he's supposed to be shipped out in the morning."

"Why?" Zoe asked, brows raised. "What's wrong with him?"

"Oh, nothing," Mac assured her. "He's the

sweetest dog. But he's been here six months and that's our limit for keeping animals before we send them to another shelter."

Mac made a slicing motion across her neck and Zoe's eyes widened. "I thought this was a no-kill shelter?"

"It is," Mac said. "So we send them to a shelter over in Boise when they don't get adopted. Since I've started working here we haven't had to send one animal to the farm. That's what I call it. I'm really good at getting people to adopt animals."

"Poor thing," Zoe said, imagining a geriatric mutt with one eye and a limp that no one wanted. "Show him to me. I don't mind an older dog. Even if he's ugly. I'm sure he'll make a great companion."

Mac led her past a kennel full of terrier puppies, a German shepherd, an English bulldog, and an assortment of mutts. They reached the very last kennel and Zoe's heart thumped wildly in her chest. She had no idea what she was looking at. A yeti or bigfoot was a possibility. She'd never seen so much white hair in her life. Not to mention he was the size of a small horse.

"It's your lucky day, Chewy," Mac said,

putting her knuckles up to the kennel gate for Chewy to sniff.

"Chewy?" Zoe asked.

"As in Chewbacca," Mac said. "'Cause he's so big and hairy."

"I can see that." Zoe felt the spit dry up in her mouth and had trouble swallowing.

"He's some kind of sheepdog mix, but he's full grown so you don't have to worry about him getting any bigger. And he's already outside trained. Though his table manners could probably use some work. But there's a great obedience school on the other side of town."

"Uh-huh," Zoe said, staring into a face with so much hair she wondered if there were eyes in there somewhere.

"I brush him every day," Mac said. "He really likes to be pampered. And he's really very sweet, and smart too. Sometimes I think he knows exactly what I'm saying. It's a little weird, actually. He only jumps when he's excited, but you've got to kind of brace yourself because he weighs more than either of us and you'll end up on the ground before you know it. But obedience school will really help him. He just doesn't realize how strong he is. How can you say no to that face? I can't even imagine him going off to the farm."

Zoe swallowed the big lump in her throat. She couldn't send Chewy to the farm. That would make her an accomplice to murder.

"Do you like condos, Chewy?" Zoe asked, tentatively reaching her hand out to let him sniff.

He woofed softly and sat politely back on his hind legs. His woof blew the hair out of his eyes long enough to see the black gaze staring back at her.

"He needs a haircut," Zoe said.

"There's a groomer not far from the obedience school. I didn't see you pull up in a car."

"I walked," Zoe said, still numb from all the life-changing decisions she'd made in less than twenty-four hours. "I live in the condo over by the lake."

"Ooh, nice," Mac said. "My cousin Hank built that development. It's very swanky. Chewy is definitely an uptown dog."

Chewy looked Zoe up and down, obviously trying to decide whether or not she passed muster, and he woofed once more before walking past them both and down the long row of kennels to the lobby door.

"Well," Zoe said. "I guess he's decided to adopt me."

Chapter Two

Colt O'Hara signed off on a chart and handed it back to his nurse. In return, she handed him the cup of coffee he so desperately needed.

His eyes were blurry and there was more than a day's worth of beard on his face. But Juliette Martin had finally delivered a healthy baby boy at seven that morning after sixteen hours of labor. Just in time for him to splash cold water on his face and be back at his office for his first appointment at eight.

He loved being a doctor. Correction…he loved being a doctor in Laurel Valley. There was a reassuring consistency in seeing to the needs of the three thousand full-time residents who lived in the resort town. And like any small-town doctor, he did a little bit of everything. There was something special about participating in the joys of a new baby, grieving with those who'd suffered loss, and going through the life stages of everything in between.

During tourist season—summer and winter— his schedule would get a little tighter. He'd treat plenty of people with altitude sickness or the common cold. But there were medics on the ski slopes and out on the lake, so anything more severe was automatically sent to the emergency room at the hospital in McCall.

"I'm heading over to The Lampstand for lunch," Lucy Hatchett said. "Going to meet my daughter. She said if she didn't get out of the house and away from the kids for a couple of hours she was going to request you sign her into the psych ward at St. Matt's so she could get a few days of peace and quiet."

Colt chuckled and stretched his neck from side to side, working out the stiffness. Hannah had graduated with his oldest brother, Duncan. She'd gotten married right out of high school to Beau Bright and then given birth to a son every year for the next five years. She'd given up on having a daughter, but had finally gotten her wish a couple of years back with a surprise package. And then

Hannah had promptly told Beau to get a vasectomy.

Lucy had been his nurse since he'd bought the practice from Doc Willis five years before. And she'd been the nurse for Doc Willis for the forty years before that. She barely stood over five feet tall, her face was wizened like a gnome, and her steel-gray hair was always perfectly set in sausage curls that lined up like soldiers across her pink scalp. She knew everyone in Laurel Valley's medical history and had it committed to memory. She gave scoldings when they were needed and lollipops to anyone under the age of twenty and over the age of sixty at every visit. He'd be lost without her.

"You go home and get some sleep," she said. "I've seen corpses that look better than you. I'll lock up here. Wally Gaines is our only afternoon appointment, but I'll give him a call and see if he can come in tomorrow morning. His gout is flared up, so it's nothing to write home about. No need to hang around here and watch the paint dry."

Closing at noon on a Wednesday sounded like a marvelous idea. And there was no use arguing with Lucy. He wouldn't have had the energy anyway. He was asleep on his feet, and then he remembered the coffee in his hand and took a sip, letting the bitterness send a jolt through his system.

"That's the best idea I've heard all week," Colt said.

"Of course it is," she said, her lips pressing together in a thin line. "You think you get to be my age without having two brain cells to rub together?"

"No, ma'am."

She hmmphed and then looked at him over the top of her glasses. "Maybe since you're so affable I should ask for a raise. Ever since your brother started building those condos and resorts the cost of living around here has gone sky high."

Colt grinned, enjoying the familiar argument. Lucy was probably the highest-paid nurse in the state and she knew it. There was a reason she hadn't retired.

"Hank's a modern-day land baron," Colt agreed. "I don't know how he keeps getting invites to Sunday dinner."

"Your mother has a soft heart," Lucy said, clucking her tongue. "Bless her. I guess it's a good thing Hank is so good looking, otherwise he wouldn't have a thing going for him."

"Which is why every single woman in west Idaho has tried to catch his attention," Colt said.

"He might as well go on one of those dating reality shows and be done with it."

Lucy hmmphed. "I haven't noticed you trying too hard to fight off all that female attention."

He gave her a grin and a wink and said, "That's because I'm a romantic at heart. I'm looking for that special someone."

She snorted out a laugh. "Don't play me, Colt O'Hara. They don't call you Dr. O'Heartthrob for nothing. Maybe the lot of you should go on a reality show together. How you all hit the genetic lottery is beyond me. But you're not fooling anyone, young man. You aren't looking to settle down or you wouldn't keep dating those empty-headed ninnyheads. This place is running smooth and steady thanks to me, you make a good living, and you're not hard on the eyes either."

Colt arched a brow. "Thank you?"

"But you're not getting any younger. I'm just saying don't waste your good years. Find a nice woman to settle down with who won't bore you to tears before dessert comes. There's something to be said for good companionship and friendship. Ed and I were married fifty years before he passed, and I still miss the sound of his voice in the mornings and the irritating way he'd chew his toast. Bless his soul."

"Hank says I'm too picky. Maybe marriage just isn't in the cards for me."

"Lord have mercy, don't let your mama hear that."

"Believe me," he said, grimacing. "The thought terrifies me. We can trace our ancestry all the way back to the Normans. There's even a story passed down through the generations about how my eleventh great-grandfather rescued one of the faeries while she was in her human form. And in true storytelling fashion, it turns out she was the daughter of the king. In repayment, the king gave my ancestor the desire of his heart, which was a wife he could love above all others for eternity."

She sighed. "Well, isn't that romantic. Maybe that's why the lot of you are so devilishly hand-some. You were kissed by the fairies."

He grinned, enjoying seeing the softer side of Lucy. "According to legend, it wasn't just my ancestor who got the gift of the wife of his heart, but every generation after. My cousins and brothers have done a good job of upholding the family legacy, but I just don't know if it's in my future. I can't even imagine myself with the woman of my heart, much less as a father with a bunch of kids. I still don't know how my parents did it. Parenthood is terrifying."

Lucy snorted. "You Irish have as much of a gift for hogwash as you do for gab. You've just spent these last years focused on the wrong things. But you're changing as you get older, and your needs and wants are changing too. Stop being such a pinhead and start looking for a real woman instead of those twenty-year-olds who only have one name."

Colt threw his head back and laughed. "Now you're starting to sound like my father."

"Mick O'Hara is no fool," Lucy said.

"Maybe I should just get a dog."

As if the universe had heard him, at that moment, the biggest, hairiest animal he'd ever seen streaked in front of the big plate-glass window of the clinic. And trailing behind it was a red leash and a woman who didn't have the sense to let it go.

Everything happened in slow motion. The papers in her hand slipped out of her grasp and scattered across the ground. She dug in her heels and bent down to pick them up, and at the same time the hairy monster put on a burst of speed that was enough to yank her off her feet and send her flying forehead first into an antique light pole. And then down for the count she went.

"Goodness gravy," Lucy whispered, horrified. "That horse-dog just deep-sixed that woman."

Colt's training kicked into gear and he ran out the front door, getting his first look at the woman sprawled on the ground. She looked young, maybe in her mid-twenties, and her skin was pale and unblemished. She had hair as short as a boy's and hadn't bothered with any makeup—she didn't need any.

He knelt down beside her to see what kind of medical attention she needed and felt for the pulse in her wrist.

She whimpered, but her eyes didn't open.

"Just take your time," Colt said. "I'm Dr. O'Hara. You're okay. You just got knocked silly."

There was no response, but he hadn't expected one. She was out cold, and a crowd was starting to gather around.

His cousin Mac ran up a few seconds later.

"Holy mackerel. Did you see that?" she asked. "Is she okay?"

"I take it you've got something to do with this?" Colt asked. "Was that Lawrence Fisher's dog I just saw MMA this woman?"

"One and the same," Mac said, her nervousness making her not let any lull in the conversation. "When Lawrence died he willed the dog to his brother, but Lionel didn't want him. And no one else wanted Chewy either because he's so big, so he got sent to us. But Lordy, you'd have thought someone shot a starting pistol at the way he took off out the door."

"Prison changes a man," Colt said dryly. "I'm sure Chewy saw his shot and went for it."

"He caught us all by surprise," Mac said. "He was as well behaved as you please before all the paperwork was signed. Then as soon as Zoe opened the door he took off and never looked back, dragging Zoe along behind him. I guess getting pardoned from death row will do that to you."

Colt grunted and said, "Her name is Zoe?"

"Zoe Green," Mac said. "She's really nice. Just moved here. She lives in one of Hank's condos. I think she's going through some stuff. Like a total life restart. But she's got great shoes and that purse is one I see in my dreams."

"Maybe we should let her wake up before you start reading me her bio," Colt said. "She just got knocked loopy. Let's get her moved into the clinic."

A shadow cast itself over Zoe, and Colt looked

up into an unrepentant face of white fur. Chewy was panting and his red leash lay on the ground beside him.

"Not the best first impression," Colt told the dog.

Chewy cocked his head and whined, and then put his giant paw on Zoe's arm.

"Does he understand what I'm saying?" Colt asked Mac.

"That seems to be the consensus," Mac said. "He's smarter than he lets on."

Chewy huffed and blew out a sigh.

Colt put his arms beneath Zoe and lifted her, surprised at how slight she was. Lucy held the door open so he could carry her inside.

"I think he's insulted," Colt said. "Better bring him inside too so he doesn't flatten anyone else."

Chewy whined again, lying down on the floor and putting his paws over his nose in embarrassment.

"Oh," Mac said, her expression sympathetic. "You hurt his feelings."

"I'll make it up to him later," Colt said. "I think our sleeping beauty is starting to wake up."

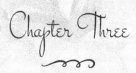

Chapter Three

There were tiny men marching inside Zoe's head. They weren't just marching, but they were wearing spiked shoes and digging their heels in every time they did an about-face. She cracked her eyes open and the light was so bright she immediately felt the nausea creep up on her.

"Light," she croaked. "Make it go away." The light disappeared.

Maybe she was dead. Maybe she'd just thwarted death by telling the light to go away. Someone was saying her name. She hated that person. Didn't they know every sound that reached her ears made the spiked shoe-wearing men give her an extra kick for good measure?

"Zoe."

"Jerk," she said, and heard someone chuckle.

"Zoe," the voice called out again.

And then she had a moment of panic. Maybe she *was* dead.

"God?" she asked tentatively.

"Gee, Colt," a familiar voice said. "That's got to be a record for you. Being called a jerk and God in the span of a few seconds."

"Happens more than you'd think," God said. "Zoe, open your eyes for me, honey. I know your head hurts."

Zoe's lashes fluttered open, and she braced herself, expecting to see the bright light again. But there was a face leaning over her instead. She had to hand it to God. He was certainly the most beautiful being she'd ever seen in her life. There was a halo of light around his face—he had gilded hair that curled slightly at the ends, a face she could only describe as one kissed by angels, and his eyes were the color of melted chocolate with the slightest golden ring around the edges.

"Beautiful," she said on a sigh. "But don't call me honey."

Was she allowed to tell God that? She wasn't sure what the protocol in a situation like this was, but she heard him chuckle and figured God had a sense of humor.

"How's your head?" he asked her.

"Hurts," she said. "Might throw up."

"I wouldn't doubt it," he said. "I'm going to shine a light in your eyes. Just need to check things out. You hit your head pretty hard."

"Mmmkay," she said. "I got a haircut."

"It looks great," God said. "Not everyone could pull a haircut like that off."

"That's what the lady at the salon said. She has a pantsuit I want. It'll make me look like a candlestick."

"What in the Sam Hill is she talking about?" Lucy asked.

"Her brains are a little scrambled," Mac said. "Is she going to be all right?"

"Nothing some ice and ibuprofen won't help," God said.

"Oh, good," Mac said. "I really like her. She's gorgeous, huh? You're going to like her too, Colt."

How many people are in the room? Zoe wondered. Two women at least. She recognized the voice of one, but she couldn't place it. And then God. And some guy named Colt. What a ridiculous name.

"I like everyone," Colt said.

"Uh, huh," Mac said. "That's why Grandma says you haven't settled down yet. You like everyone *too* much."

"I'm glad to know my love life is the topic of everyone's conversations," Colt said.

"It's because we love you. Everyone just wants you to be happy. And I'm telling you I think Zoe is the one. I've got a special talent for these things, you know? I'm good at matchmaking. Grandma says it's because I've got extra Irish in me."

"You're good with matching people with animals," Colt said. "I'm pretty sure you're batting zero for matching people with people."

"Well, it can't be too much different," she said. "I get the same feeling in my gut either way."

"Speaking of guts," Lucy said. "Do you need me here for this? My stomach is starting to growl. I'm an old lady. I've got to eat regular."

"Head on out and say hi to your daughter for me," Colt said.

"Huckleberry pie is on the menu today," Mac said.

"You don't have to tell me twice," Lucy said. "Your grandma makes the best huckleberry pie in the state."

"I didn't expect heaven to be so informal," Zoe said, but the thought of pie put her over the edge. "Gonna throw up now." And she did.

———

When her eyes opened again she had a little more clarity about her surroundings and a vague memory of a hairy dog and a metal lamppost.

She groaned and tried to sit up, but her brain wasn't sending the right signals to her body.

"Take it slow and easy."

She recognized the voice. It had been prevalent in the nightmare she'd just had where she'd met the most attractive man she'd ever seen and then thrown up all over him.

Zoe groaned and then said, "Sorry I threw up on you."

He chuckled. "I've had a lot worse. I'm Colt O'Hara, by the way. You're just lucky you had your accident right in front of my clinic. I was able to get to you quickly."

"So I'm not dead?" she asked.

"Nope," he answered. "And I'm not God. Just the town doctor."

"I figured as much," she said on a sigh. There was an ice pack on her forehead and it slipped down to her nose when she turned her head. "Ohmigosh. I'm the worst dog mother ever. I didn't even last thirty seconds before he got away from me."

"Don't worry," Colt said. "Chewy didn't go far. In fact, he told me he feels really bad about what happened to you. I gave him my leftover sandwich from the fridge to console him."

"He told you?" Zoe asked.

"In a manner of speaking. He's a good communicator."

Zoe pressed the ice pack to her forehead and gingerly sat up. "I need to get home. I've had more excitement than I can stand for one day."

"Mac said you live over in the new condos by the lake," Colt said.

"Mac?" Zoe asked, and then she remembered. "Oh, Mac. Where is she? Was she here or did I dream that?"

"She was here," Colt said. "She had to go back to work, but she said she'd check on you later. You should really stay lying down."

But he took her elbow to steady her as she ignored the suggestion and pushed off the exam table to get to her feet.

"Can't," she said. "Need to get home. Got work to do."

"Uh-huh," he said. "You're going to be woozy for a while. You might ought to take the rest of the day off. If you don't want to lie down, at least sit down. Let me get you some water."

Her vision swam and her stomach went queasy. She had to get away from this man. She'd already embarrassed herself enough.

"No," she insisted. "I want to go home. I've sworn off men."

"Ha!" Colt said. "I didn't realize we'd moved to the dating part of our relationship."

"Sorry," she said, closing her eyes and taking a deep breath to settle her stomach. "My brain isn't forming the words I want to come out of my mouth."

"I'm good at reading between the lines," he said, taking her elbow again when she wobbled. "You must have seen me from afar and found me unbearably handsome. So you decided the fastest way to get into my arms was by giving yourself a concussion on my sidewalk. And now that you've been on my exam table you've decided you've bit off more than you can chew. I make you nervous. I guess Mac is right. We're destined to be together. She's a matchmaker you know."

She groaned again. "So I've been told." Her head was swimming with his nonsense. "O'Hara." His name rang a distant bell. "Are you and Mac related?"

"Yeah," Colt said. "Mac is my cousin Ryder's daughter. So she's my second cousin. Good kid."

"I would have known you were related without the last name. I've heard two of the most ridiculous stories today I've heard in my lifetime. You could both give me a run for my money in the storytelling department."

"Ahh, well," he said. "That's because the O'Haras come from a long line of *seanchai.*"

"Are you going to make me ask what that is? Because my head really hurts."

"The *seanchai* are ancient Irish storytellers."

"Figures," she said. "I think you're both full of blarney. It must be nice to have family close by."

"It has its moments," he said. "If you're going to be stubborn at least let me give you a ride home. In fact, I insist on it. I can't in good conscience leave you to your own devices. You might end up in the lake."

"As an independent female, I'd normally decline that invitation," she said. "But I'm willing to set the feminist movement back a few years and accept your hospitality."

"Nothing wrong with having common sense, no matter who you are. And because you've already forfeited your feminist duties, I'll just go ahead and insist you let me wheel you out in this wheelchair. My Bronco is parked right out back."

He easily pushed her down into the wheelchair that was sitting outside the exam room. Sweat had started to bead at her brow from the exertion of walking across the room.

"I'm going to be really mad about this later," she said. "I'm an independent woman. I'm starting a new adventure."

"I'd call a concussion a new adventure," Colt said, shaking his head. This was why he dated empty-headed ninnyheads, as Lucy had called them. Zoe Green had a head as hard as a rock. "What you need is ice and rest. Do you have anyone to help you out? Are you married?"

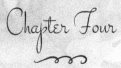

Chapter Four

COLT WASN'T SURE WHY HE'D ASKED HER THAT question. Only that he found it important to get an answer. Not only an answer, but the answer he wanted to hear. He must be more tired than he thought.

She had backbone, he'd give her that. It had been sheer force of will that had allowed her to walk from one side of the room to the other.

"No," she said. "I'm not married. Not anymore."

"Ahh," he said. Colt could infer that her new adventure and independence might have something to do with that. "Do you have any family or friends in the area? Someone who could check on you?"

"No, no one." Her voice was monotone, without any emotion. "It's just me and Chewy."

"That's no trouble," he said, keeping his voice light and cheerful.

He'd always been dubbed the O'Hara who was never in a bad mood. It was his gift. Which he'd learned partnered well with his healing abilities. Because he always managed to deliver bad news to his patients with an encouraging word so they left hopeful for their future.

"I've been known to do house calls from time to time," he said. "I can stop by and check on you before work and between patients."

"That's really not necessary," she said.

"It really is," he said, grinning into her scowling face. "You've got a concussion and a nice-sized lump on your head. Things can turn serious with head trauma. And as resourceful as Chewy seems to be, I don't think nursing duties are on his resume."

"Are you always this cheerful?" she asked, frowning.

"Pretty much."

"It's really annoying."

He stifled a laugh, enjoying the conversation with her more than he had with anyone in a long while. He could only imagine what it would be like when she was at her full strength.

"I'll try to be less happy," he said. "Come on, Chewy. It's the back seat for you. Up."

Colt opened the back door of his restored classic Bronco and Chewy jumped inside.

"How'd you get him to do that?" she asked. "Obey your command?"

She pushed herself up out of the wheelchair and held on to the door to get her balance. "I told him to stop and sit just before he ran me into that pole and I saw stars."

Chewy whined and raised a paw toward her. She would have felt like a heel for not acknowledging the gesture, so she shook the furry foot politely. And then she bit back a comment as Colt practically lifted her into the passenger seat. He was just trying to help, and in all honesty she appreciated it. She would have given everything she had just to lie down where she was and drift off into endless sleep.

"I mean it about the concussion," he said. "You've really got to take it easy for the next few days. And I'm going to make sure you do. If I see you out window-shopping or eating lunch at The Lampstand I'm going to call the sheriff and have you hauled back home."

"Is that how the cops get their kicks around here?" she asked, closing her eyes as he backed out of the parking spot. Her stomach lurched dangerously. "Laurel Valley doesn't look like the kind of place that sees much action. I bet the cops get bored."

"There's more action than you'd think," Colt said. "My cousin Blaze is the sheriff."

"Of course he is," she said. "Chewy and I aren't afraid of the law. Right Chewy?"

Chewy whined and made a strange sound as if he were trying to form words. And then he followed it up with a single bark.

"Chewy knows better than to get on the wrong side of the law."

"This dog has secrets," Zoe said, shaking her head. "He's lived a life. He knows things."

Colt smiled. "Wouldn't surprise me at all. Chewy here was Lawrence Fisher's dog. Lawrence was a Vietnam veteran and a local hunting guide. He was a survivor. So I wouldn't be surprised if Chewy could do everything from gutting a fish to building a bomb."

"And how did Lawrence's dog end up as a ward of the state?"

"Well," Colt said. "Old Lawrence was out on one of his ramblings. That's what the locals called them. It wasn't unusual for him to be gone days at a time. But he dropped dead of a heart attack while he was in the mountains and Chewy came into town and went straight to the police and led them back to Lawrence."

"Oh, how awful," Zoe said. "Poor baby."

Chewy whined again and laid his massive head on her shoulder.

Colt knew he was a goner. All he could hear was the blood rushing in his ears and his heart thudding in his chest. If a neon sign had been hanging over her head flashing, *This One,* he wouldn't have been surprised at all.

The look of love on Zoe's face was so plain and pure, he wondered if Chewy knew exactly how lucky he was. Gone was the rigid exterior she'd been exuding and in its place was a softness and yearning to love and be loved. He wanted her to look at him like she was looking at Chewy.

Colt had heard the stories from his father and grandfather about how it had only taken one look to recognize the one for them. His heart turned over in his chest, and for the first time ever he could see his future in this woman—a complete stranger—and it didn't bother him in the slightest. He rolled his window down to let the cool breeze bring him back to his senses before he said something his tired brain would regret later.

"Chewy is a lucky dog," he told her.

"You don't know how lucky," she said. "If he was a gambling sort he'd have won the jackpot."

"Too bad gambling is illegal for dogs in Idaho," Colt said dryly.

"Are you sure you're a doctor?"

"As opposed to what?"

"A stand-up comedian or a serial killer."

"Is one considered worse than the other?" he asked.

"The jury is still out. You should stop talking. You're making my head hurt."

Her bluntness made him chuckle. Yep, he was a goner all right. She fascinated him. He was attracted to her on a physical level. How could he not be? She was beautiful, just as Mac had said. But she had a sharp wit and a keen mind, and he'd enjoyed their short conversation so far. She was probably a force to be reckoned with when she wasn't half addled.

Colt rubbed his eyes and shook his head. He needed a nap.

"You okay?" she asked, eyeing him warily.

"Yeah, just short on sleep," he said. "What was I saying?"

"You'd originally started telling me about Chewy's owner, but then you got a look in your eyes like you'd been hit with a frying pan. Boy, can I pick 'em," she said, glumly.

"Hey, I'm a great catch," he said. "I promise I'll show you once you're not concussed. Now stop interrupting and let me finish my story."

She made a sound that had Chewy's ears perking up, but Colt just smiled and kept talking.

"Anyway, after Lawrence's funeral, an attorney showed up and read the will. Old Lawrence didn't have too much to leave in the way of possessions. He was a simple man, and all he had was his cabin, an old pickup truck, and Chewy. Lawrence's brother got the cabin and pickup and sold them both right away. But he didn't want to take Chewy back to Boise with him. Said he didn't have time to take care of a dog."

"And now he's mine," Zoe said, rubbing Chewy's fur affectionately. "Now he's an uptown dog. That's my garage space." She pointed to the two-car garage. "You can pull into the driveway. Thank you for the ride."

She opened the door and hopped down before he could come around and help her. Then her knees buckled and she slid down to the ground gracefully.

He rolled his eyes and said, "Lord give me strength to deal with stubborn women."

"I heard that," she said.

"I wasn't trying to keep it a secret," he said, hurrying around to the other side of the car. It was faster to carry her, so that's exactly what he did. And then he opened the back door so Chewy could get out, who proceeded to trot over to the closest patch of grass to do his business.

She rested her head against his chest, and he thought she felt just right in his arms. This was a dangerous woman. He couldn't wait to see how dangerous.

"Are you good at taking advice?" he asked.

"Not particularly," she said, making his lips twitch. "I'm on a deadline."

"What kind of deadline?"

"A book deadline," she said. "I write novels for women. A brave heroine, a little action and adventure, and then toss in a life-shattering event in an unusual location or time period and you have the keys to happily-ever-after."

"Hmm," Colt said. "That makes sense. And you did say you were a storyteller. Though your cynicism would lend itself well to crime novels I think. You seem like the kind of person who could think of creative ways to murder someone."

"Thank you?"

"It's a compliment. I like your brain."

"You're not going to make a crack about the kinds of books I write?"

He looked at her quizzically. "Why would I make a crack about what you write? The best stories are ones about relationships. Every ancient text, book, and movie on the planet is about relationships. I take it you deal with that kind of stuff a lot?"

She let out a breath and he realized she'd been steeling herself for a reaction different than he gave.

"You could say that," she said. "There's not a lot of respect for women writers in the literary world."

"By the looks of you and this condo," he said. "I'm sure you're laughing about that lack of respect all the way to the bank. And I don't think you're going to have to worry too much about your deadline over the next couple of days."

"Why's that?" she asked.

He carried her into a plush lobby with a large river rock fireplace, a comfortable seating area in soft greens and gold, and a row of gold-plated mailboxes in the wall that were neatly numbered.

"Because staring at tiny words on the screen is

not going to be fun," he told her. "Best thing to do is just close your eyes, embrace the ice pack, and get the sleep your body is going to demand."

"You might be right," she said. "I've never had a concussion before. I wasn't expecting my move here to be so hazardous to my health."

They got into the elevator and Chewy trotted in behind them, sitting politely at Colt's feet as they made their way up to the top floor.

"Civilized dog," she said, reaching an arm down and patting Chewy on the top of the head. "Am I getting too heavy for you?"

"Of course not," he said. "What kind of man would I be if I admitted you were too heavy? That's a recipe for disaster. You either poison my bagel because I called you too heavy or you question my manhood because I'm a weakling."

"I see your point," she said. "It is a pickle. I withdraw the question."

"Very kind of you," he said. "I'm assuming you have a key in that purse of yours? Or am I going to have to pick the locks?"

"A doctor who picks locks?" she asked. Her voice was slurred with exhaustion and she reminded him of a toddler who kept talking just to stay awake. "Interesting hobbies you have."

"I also play the piano and the occasional

game of golf, but my golf game leaves a lot to be desired."

"You can't have it all," she said.

"Tell me about it."

The elevator door opened into an opulent private foyer. He knew how expensive these condos were. He'd considered buying this very one for himself when Hank had given the family a tour early on in the build phase. One thing was for sure, Zoe Green had money. A lot of it.

What was a woman with her talents and resources doing in Laurel Valley? She didn't have local family or friends, she wasn't married, and for whatever reason she'd felt the need to reinvent herself and hit the start button on a new life. She'd used the word independence a couple of times in their short time together. What had kept her so chained that she'd yearned for freedom and independence with that kind of focused determination?

He set her gently on her feet and she removed her keys from the clip on her purse and opened the door. He followed her inside and closed the door behind him.

"Gorgeous," he said, enjoying the view that looked out over a lake so clear it looked like glass. It was framed by white-capped mountains and towering pines. "I was almost tempted to buy this exact condo because of that view."

"That would have thrown a wrench in my plan," she said. "The other ones on this side have great views, but not like this. I knew the second I saw the pictures I'd do whatever it took to make it mine."

"I'm sure Hank loved that," Colt said. "Didn't you have a Realtor or someone to keep you from getting taken to the cleaners?"

"Are you saying your brother is a swindler?"

"No, Hank's as honest as they come," Colt said immediately. "But I hope you negotiated a little. Just out of principle."

"I offered full price right off the bat," she said, moving toward the big L-shaped white couch in the middle of the room, but she didn't sit down.

There were boxes stacked against all the walls, some opened, others still sealed shut, and there were no personal items set about. Living out of boxes for a week would have driven him crazy. His family—bless them—were all organized souls. His mother had taught her boys from a young age that mess belonged out in the pasture and never in the house. And heaven help them all if they tracked dirt inside or let muddy dogs run through her kitchen. They hadn't loved those lessons as children, but Colt had to admit it had served him well through medical school and when he'd moved out on his own.

"I didn't want to take the chance that someone might outbid me," she said. "Besides, it's a reasonable price compared to where I'm from. But it's a shame we're not neighbors. It would have made your house calls a little easier. So... why weren't you tempted?

His gaze met hers and his breath caught in his chest. There was something electric sizzling between them, and it took every ounce of control he had not to walk over to her and see if her lips were as soft as they looked. If she'd been holding an apple he would have taken a bite and said to heck with the consequences.

He realized he was taking too long to answer and he ran back the conversation through his mind so he had a clue what she was talking about.

She arched a brow knowingly and smirked. Good. She'd felt it too. That would save some time in the future.

"Why wasn't I tempted to take this place?" he asked. "Too much of a commitment, maybe. A place like this needs great furniture and art. It needs to be filled with music and parties and laughter. I don't have a lot of time for that stuff. I live above the clinic. It's more efficient and easier if I'm needed in an emergency."

"Ahh," she said. "I recognize another workaholic when I see one. What do you do to relax?"

"Oh, I'm great at relaxing," he said, grinning. "Are you going to lie down on the couch, or are you going to stand there until you fall down? Lord, you must have a head as hard as a rock. Maybe I need to be checking the light post for damage."

She blew out a sigh. "Fine, I'm lying down. Happy now?"

"Yes, that's much better," he said. "Keep that ice on your head."

"You were bragging about how great you are at relaxing," she prodded. "Must be nice."

"Oh, it is," he said. "It's another O'Hara family trait. We are all passionate about our work. And it's easy for us to be consumed by it if we let ourselves. My brother Duncan is an artist. Sometimes he'll be in his studio for days at a time. Hank is a developer and owns his own construction business, as you know. My brother Aidan and his wife own their own mechanic shop, but he specializes in working on high-dollar cars like Ferrari and Porsche. And then there's my youngest brother, Wyatt. He works for the DEA.

He's gone a lot and doesn't really tell us a whole lot."

"Good grief," she said. "How many brothers do you have?"

"There's five of us total," he said. "And my uncle and aunt have five too. Plus my grandparents and various nieces and nephews. There are a lot of us."

"They don't mention it on the Laurel Valley Wikipedia page."

He chuckled and said, "I'm starting to enjoy that smart mouth of yours."

"I'm sure you'll get tired of it soon enough," she said, closing her eyes.

Colt raised his brows at that. Must be something of a sore spot, but he decided to deflect the conversation and keep telling her about his family. She'd meet them all soon enough. He'd make sure of that.

"What I'm saying," he said, "is that we all tend to be obsessed with our work. But when it's time to play, we play hard."

"Is this where piano and golf come in?"

"Mmmhmm," he said. "I've also got a cabin in the mountains." He found a folded throw on top of one of the boxes and laid it over her. "My family owns a good part of the east side of the

51

mountain and the lake, and we all inherited enough acreage so we could build our own places and leave land for our own children to inherit."

"Someone planned ahead," she said.

"That would be my great-grandfather," Colt said. "He came here from Ireland to find his fortune, and find his fortune he did. Turns out he had a way with thoroughbreds and built himself quite a stable of champions. My grandfather and my dad have continued on that legacy."

"You're lucky," she said. "Not everyone has a legacy."

"No," he agreed. "But everyone can start one. My cabin is nestled right behind that ridge down there on the other side of the lake. There's another lake that's smaller than this one, and it's on O'Hara land. The fishing and water-skiing are great, and I have a hammock that has the ability to make a person fall asleep within seconds. It's my escape when I'm able to get away."

"And what do you need to escape from?" she asked, snuggling down under the covers.

"Beautiful women knocking themselves sense-less so they can get me in their apartment," he said teasingly.

"If I had the energy I'd throw something at you," she said.

"Well, I'm disappointed to miss that. I'm sure you have quite the throwing arm. When I first saw you I thought to myself, she must play softball. I know an athlete when I see one."

"Shut up," she said, chuckling. "You are so annoying."

"So you said before. You also told me I was too cheerful."

"I liked it better when I thought I was dead and you were God."

"We can role-play later," he said. "You'll need your full strength for that."

"Maybe I could escape to your cabin," she said. "Just for some peace and quiet. And maybe some Advil."

He chuckled and said, "I'm getting it. And you can use the cabin anytime you'd like. It's been almost a year since I've been able to get away. Laurel Valley isn't as small as it used to be, and I rarely go a week without a call in the middle of the night or the weekend.

"Why don't you hire another doctor?" she asked.

"I'll have to before the year is out," he said. "But there's more money to be made at the hospitals outside of Laurel Valley. Most doctors don't want to move to the middle of nowhere to work terrible hours and make a lot less than they would at the hospital."

"The right person will come along exactly when you need them," she said. "There's a lot to be said for getting to live in a place like this. Terrible hours and less pay are sometimes worth it for peace of mind."

"Hmm," he said. "Sounds like you're speaking from experience."

She yawned and closed her eyes. "Thanks for seeing me home. You've gone above and beyond the call of doctorly duties. Can you turn the light out when you leave? My eyes hurt."

Colt snorted. Her conversation diversion wasn't subtle at all.

"Here's your hat, what's your hurry?" he asked. "Don't worry. I'll be out of your hair soon enough."

He did as she asked and turned the overhead lights off, but sunlight was streaming through the expanse of windows. There was nothing he could do about that.

"I'm going to get you a fresh ice pack and ibuprofen before I leave," he said. "If you have any."

"Of course I do," she said. "I'm a writer. Look in the kitchen. It's right next to the coffee maker."

It was a large condo, two floors, and as much square footage as his cabin. Downstairs consisted of an open floor plan, a large commercial kitchen in white with gold hardware and fixtures, and a dining area with a modern glass table and eight chairs. He thought it ironic she'd have a space built for entertaining when she knew absolutely no one and didn't seem like the type to invite them in.

He maneuvered his way through to the kitchen, and he noticed there was one area of the house she had set up—her office. He didn't feel bad about peeking inside. The French doors were wide open.

Priorities. He understood them. His clinic had been the first thing he'd started renovations on when he'd bought Doc Willis's practice. She had a sleek desk made of the same glass as the dining room table and there was a desktop computer with two monitors on its surface. There was a treadmill in the corner and shelves filled with everything from research books to ornately carved knives, awards, and a whimsical glass dragon.

But in front of the large picture window was an old comfortable chair, a single floor lamp, and a leopard-print throw that had seen better days but looked very soft. He knew instinctively this was her real workspace.

He moved into the kitchen and almost laughed. Again, priorities. The countertops were completely bare except for a very fancy coffee machine and a giant mug. Next to the mug was a Costco-sized bottle of ibuprofen.

"How long have you lived here?" Colt asked.

"Exactly one week," she said. "Why?"

"You have no food."

"I have cereal in that box over there. And milk and a bottle of wine in the fridge. I order in for everything else. At least for now until I get the kitchen set up. I don't spend a lot of time cooking."

"I'd never have guessed," he said under his breath. "Keep that ice on your head. It'll help the swelling go down. But you're going to be an interesting shade of green and purple for the next few days."

"Good thing I don't know anyone," she said. "It might raise questions."

"I'm pretty sure everyone in town already knows who you are, what happened to you, and where you live. The locals don't miss much."

He grabbed a bottle of water and four ibuprofen and went back into the living area.

Chewy had made himself at home on the chair next to his new mistress.

"You didn't know who I was," she said irritably.

"That's because I've delivered four babies, given a hundred physicals for the upcoming athletic season at the high school, and treated twenty-two summer colds over the last week. And I haven't seen any of my family. They're my normal gossip dealers."

She took the ibuprofen and water from him. "You were too busy to see them or you chose not to see them?"

"Strategic avoidance," he said, grinning. "I've become quite adept. Do you have plastic bags? I'll make you another ice pack before I go and refreeze this one."

"They're in a box," she said, waving her hand toward an open box. "I only know that because I was looking for the cereal and I came across them."

Her voice was trailing off, and he could see the dark circles of exhaustion beneath her eyes. He found the plastic bags and filled one with ice, and then he found a dish towel and wrapped it around the bag, switching it out for the one she was holding on her forehead.

"Get some sleep," he said. "Chewy will watch over you. And I'll be back to check on you and bring you something to eat. It can be our first date."

She mumbled something unintelligible and he took it as a sign of acknowledgement before telling Chewy goodbye and letting himself out the door.

It had been quite the day. And if he didn't get some sleep he wouldn't have the energy to pry all the secrets out of the woman who he knew would be the wife of his heart.

Chapter Five

ZOE HAD HATED BEING MARRIED. OR MAYBE SHE'D just hated being married to Todd. But it's not like her parents hadn't given her a roadmap for the misery of marriage in the first place. Why she'd chosen to ignore everything she'd seen with her own eyes and chosen to believe that things would be different with Todd still confounded her. She could only chalk it up to a temporary lack of sanity.

Maybe her bad decisions had just been a moment of crisis as she'd turned thirty. So she'd let Todd sweep her up in the romance of it all, not paying any attention to the red flags that had been waving right in her face—like the fact she'd never been to his apartment or hadn't known exactly what he did for a living. *Consultant* covered a lot of bases. Mostly unemployed freeloader in her experience.

The honeymoon phase wore off after the first three months. She'd spent the next six months trying to figure out how to untangle herself from the situation. And then she'd spent the next two years fighting for her livelihood and not letting him walk out with everything she'd worked for. But in the end the judge had ruled that she didn't have to give him half of her intellectual property rights of every book she'd ever written. But she'd had to make some concessions for her freedom.

She stared at the text he'd sent and felt the knot in her stomach. For the next five years she'd be tied to him. He wanted his alimony payment early, because lo and behold, he was already out of money from last month's deposit.

She did a couple of deep-breathing exercises that her therapist had suggested and felt the rage that came along whenever she had to deal with Todd dissipate. From the moment they met until the moment she'd kicked him out, they'd known each other less than a year. He was but a small blip in her life. But it was amazing how just the sight of his name popping up on her phone could incite such a reaction.

Once the rage left and the blood stopped pounding in her ears, it was replaced with the headache that had nagged her through a fitful sleep. There was a whine to her right and she tried to stretch her neck to see where it was coming from. And then she remembered. She had a dog.

"Well, Chewy," she said, stretching out the kinks in her back. "I guess I haven't given you much of a welcome. Thank you for not chewing up my furniture."

He gave a soft woof and then unfolded his enormous body from the chair and padded toward her.

"You're a little bigger than I had in mind when I decided to get a dog," she confessed, scratching him behind the ears. "What did your owner feed you? Maybe we ought to cut it back a little."

He growled low in his throat and turned his back on her. And then his head cocked to the side and he gave out a different kind of bark—almost a warning.

Zoe would have rolled her eyes, but her head was hurting too bad. Leave it to her to end up with a dog who thought he was human. And a man at that. In her experience, you couldn't teach an old dog new tricks once they were set in their ways.

Her stomach rumbled and Chewy gave her an embarrassed look.

"Hey, I haven't eaten all day," she told him. "A little less judgment please. A lot has happened today. My divorce was finalized this morning. Imagine that, after two years it's finally over. And then to celebrate I got a haircut."

She touched the back of her neck as she sat up on the couch, marveling at the feel of nothing but skin. "You don't know what a big deal that is because you didn't know me before, but believe me, I look very different than I did yesterday."

Chewy woofed again and Zoe said, "Thank you," deciding he was giving her a compliment.

"And then I got you," she said. "And you know what happened after that."

Chewy lay down on the floor and covered his face with his paws, whining.

"I forgive you," Zoe said. "You were just excited. But we've got to work on listening to commands. I can't go around with concussions all the time. That's not conducive to creative book ideas."

The sun was still up, but she could tell by the positioning over the mountains that it was late afternoon. She'd been asleep a few hours at least. And she wondered if it was too soon to take more ibuprofen.

Just as she'd swung her legs to the floor there was a knock at the door.

"Oh, no," she said, looking at Chewy wide eyed. "I bet it's the sexy doctor. They do not make doctors like that in New York. And what's up with all the cheerfulness? I mean, who doesn't get in a bad mood from time to time? Can you even trust a person who's that good natured? The answer is no. There's no man out there who's just that 'nice.' With the exception of you, of course."

Chewy made a sound like he was gargling marbles and padded over to the door, putting his paw on the knob like he was going to open it.

"Wait!" Zoe hissed. "Chewy, no. I've got to think. Dr. O'Hara is a scoundrel." It sounded better in her head if she didn't call him by his first name. She didn't want to become too familiar. "I write about these men in my books, so I know how to recognize one. You'll just have to trust me on that."

Chewy put his paw down and looked at her like she was crazy.

"Did you see the way he looked at me when I asked him why he wasn't tempted? You'd have thought we were standing naked in the garden with the serpent. I almost passed out on the spot. Do think he's married?" She waved her hand in dismissal. "It doesn't matter anyway because I've sworn off men forever."

There was another knock at the door, and Zoe figured it would be rude not to answer. He knew she was here. Besides, he was a doctor, and he'd taken an oath to do no harm. And she wouldn't put it past him to let himself in if she ignored him. He was a scoundrel after all.

─────

Colt heard the knock on his door somewhere in his subconscious and groaned. It wasn't often he regretted living in the quarters above the clinic, but this was one of those times. He scrubbed his hands over his eyes and put his feet on the pine floor. He looked at his phone for the time and grunted. He'd had five full hours of sleep. That was more than he'd had the last two days combined.

"I've got homemade lasagna," his mother's voice called out through the door.

He grinned and scrubbed his hands over his face. The fan whirred over the king-sized bed and he clicked the remote so the shades rolled up and let in the sunlight. He pulled on a pair of soft flannel pants and a white T-shirt and padded his way through the apartment to the door.

"I figured that would get you to open up," Anne O'Hara said, grinning up at him in triumph.

He'd been taller than her since the seventh grade, but she'd always been a force to be reckoned with. She was petite in stature and mighty in presence, which had served her well on the stage. She'd started her career on Broadway before she'd taken one look at Mick O'Hara and followed him halfway across the country. Her red hair wasn't as vibrant as it had once been, but her eyes were still as blue and clear as ever. And they didn't miss much.

He took the lasagna and set it down and then wrapped her in a hug. The top of her head barely came to his chest.

"Ahh," she said. "This makes all those hours in the kitchen slaving over my homemade red sauce worth it. I've missed your hugs."

"It's been a busy week," he said.

"So I've heard." She looked him over from head to toe like only a mother could do. "You look like something the cat dragged in. I'm sorry I woke you. I'll make it a quick visit so you can go back to bed."

"No, it's fine. I needed to get up. I have patients to see to tonight."

"Hmm," Anne said, taking the lasagna and making her way toward the kitchen.

On the way she did a quick glance through the living area, whether she was looking for untidiness or signs of a woman he wasn't sure, but it made him smile anyway. His mother was, after all, still a mother. It didn't matter how old he got.

He inhaled the fragrant aroma of the lasagna and followed her into the kitchen. The evening sun glowed orange through the west windows in the living room and gleamed off the large island in his kitchen. It made him think of Zoe and her bare counters. Unlike her, he loved to cook and made good use of the appliances in the renovated kitchen. Fresh herbs grew on his windowsill and earthen stoneware was stacked in his cabinets.

"I didn't realize how hungry I was until I smelled your cooking," he said, taking a seat on a barstool while she made herself at home in the kitchen. "I didn't get a chance to eat lunch. Or breakfast," he added as an afterthought.

"I'm not surprised," she said. "I heard Juliette Martin finally delivered her baby."

"Nine pounds, nine ounces," Colt said. "It was a long and rough one."

She put on a pot of coffee and took two mugs from the hook. "Your bananas are going bad."

"I haven't had time to go to the store. Or eat them."

"You don't have to be a hero, you know," she said, leaning across the island and putting her hand to the side of his face. "All you have to do is call and help will always be on the way."

He took her hand with his own and kissed it. "I know it. And I love you for it. But that's just life. It gets busy and we all just go along as best we can."

"When did I get old enough to have a son with that kind of wisdom?"

"Just because you don't recognize *your* birthdays doesn't mean the rest of us stopped."

"Brat," she said, laughing and swatting his hand away. "And just because you've decided to be ornery, I'll tell you I know you haven't just been delivering babies today." She poured the coffee into the mugs and then pursed her lips. "I hear she's very pretty."

"Ha!" Colt said. "Let me guess. Mac told Aunt Simone about the woman who got knocked out in front of the clinic. And then Simone called you. And you figured you'd sweeten me up with a home-cooked meal so you could find out more about her."

She answered his grin with one of her own, but didn't deny it. "It's not every day we get new blood in Laurel Valley. Raven told Simone the woman is single."

"Raven knows her too?" Colt asked, though he wasn't surprised.

Raven's boutique was in the heart of downtown Laurel Valley. It was highly trafficked and very popular among locals and tourists. And his Aunt Simone owned The Lampstand. Between the two of them, there wasn't much that went past their notice.

"They were in the salon this morning at the same time," Anne said. "Raven said she really felt for the girl. She said beneath all that confidence and bravado is someone who is hurting deeply."

"Raven got all that from a hair appointment?" Colt asked. He took a sip of the coffee his mother handed him while she doctored hers with enough cream and sugar that it couldn't really be called coffee anymore. He'd learned to drink it black in medical school and he'd never gotten out of the habit. The caffeine brought a much-needed jolt to his system.

"You know how intuitive Raven is," she said, shrugging. "I heard the girl hit her head pretty hard. Is she okay?"

"Her name is Zoe," Colt said. "And yes, she's okay. Just a concussion. And a nice-sized lump on her forehead. She adopted Lawrence Fisher's dog and he got away from her."

"Rest his soul," Anne said. "I couldn't believe his own brother sold all his belongings and took the money from the sale, and then sent that poor dog to the shelter. I told your father we could take him, but after the baby goat episode he said I can't bring any more animals home."

Colt hid his smirk behind his coffee cup. The year before his mother had decided what their ranch needed was baby goats. She was going to open up goat yoga at the ranch and make a killing. But the goats had caused more mischief than they were worth. They'd figured out how to open the pens and let the horses out, and they liked to sneak in through the dog door and help themselves to the food in the kitchen.

"Well, the dog has a good home now," Colt said. "They'll be good company for each other. I think they're both lonely."

"And what do you think about her?" Anne asked, arching a brow.

"I think she's my patient," Colt said. "And that she has a concussion."

"Raven said she was beautiful," Anne said. "And that she's freshly divorced."

"Fascinating," Colt said, his eyes wide. "And what else did the local gossips say? You know that's a sin, right? I'm going to tell Reverend Hughes you and Simone are at the center of a major gossip ring, and I bet he'll make a whole sermon about you like that time when Joe Donnelly was cheating on his wife and he called him out right in the middle of service."

"Hmm," Anne said primly. "It's not gossip when you're looking out for your favorite next to youngest son's future. I'm just saying, maybe don't count her out because she's your patient. You're not getting any younger you know."

"Count her out for what?" he asked, pinning her down.

She rapped him lightly on the side of the head and said, "For a wife, fool. You're too old to keep dating those sorority girls and nitwits."

"You're the second person today to tell me what you think about the women I've dated," he said, narrowing his eyes.

"Well then, it must be true," she said sweetly. "Maybe this woman is exactly what you need. My only desire is that all my children are happy and healthy. The desires of *your* heart are the desires of my heart."

She took his hand and squeezed it gently. His parents had always been a stable constant in his life. They'd nurtured, loved, corrected, laughed, and released him and his four brothers into adulthood knowing they would always have the support of the O'Hara family behind them. And they'd always given him and his brothers the room to make mistakes and learn from them.

"Well," he said, his voice husky. "It just so happens I've already come to that conclusion. And I think you'll like her very much. She's stubborn and has a quick wit, and she's not afraid to tell you what she thinks. And I have every intention of taking a shower and then taking this lasagna over to her place to see how my patient is holding up."

"And maybe this time she won't throw up on your shoes," Anne said, winking. She took his empty cup and rinsed them both in the sink before she put them in the dishwasher.

"It's scary how fast word travels," he said, shaking his head. "You and Simone should be ashamed of yourselves, making Mac one of your informants. It's bad enough you have Raven at the boutique, Dylan at the mechanic shop, and Hattie at the sporting goods store. Do you really need to bring a kid into your nefarious ring of busybodies?"

"Oh, stop it," she said, laughing. "It's not my fault everyone is so well placed in the community. They're just there, going about their business, and things happen right in front of them. That's no one's fault. Besides, we're a founding family. It's our duty to stay informed so we can care for those in the community."

"Mmmhmm," he said. "That's a nice spin. You should stick with that one."

"Thank you," Anne said. "Well, my work here is done. You need to take care of yourself. You're working too much and too hard. And call your brothers. They're all worried about you."

"Yes, that sounds like them," Colt said, laughing. "But I'll be there for dinner after church on Sunday."

Anne smiled, pleased with the announcement, and then she gave him a hug and let herself out. No doubt to go share what she'd learned with Aunt Simone. Colt laughed and headed to the shower. Maybe he could talk Zoe into Sunday dinner.

Chapter Six

COLT DIDN'T KNOW WHY HE FELT SO NERVOUS. HE was never nervous around women. One of his gifts was that he was good with people—it's one of the reasons he felt called to be a family doctor instead of taking the surgeon's position he'd been offered after his residency.

His way with people who needed medical care wasn't his only gift. He'd been using his ability to sense moods and the subtle nuances of women since his teenage years. He'd never had a challenge where a woman was concerned, not that he was necessarily looking for one, but his father had always said that the right woman wouldn't make things so easy. And that's how he'd know she was the right one.

Colt pressed the button that led to the top

floor of the building and waited impatiently as music played softly on the ride up. He'd told her he was coming back and that he'd bring dinner with him. He was a doctor and she was a patient.

Besides, the state of her kitchen was pitiful. And maybe he could help her unpack. Having boxes stacked about would have driven him crazy. His apartment was ruthlessly organized and neat. He'd learned that emergencies didn't wait for the doctor to find his car keys or shoes. It was best to always know where everything was.

He knocked and heard several barks followed by laughter. His brow furrowed. Why did he hear laughter? Jealousy gripped at his stomach, but he shook it off quickly. That wasn't like him at all, and he didn't know where the feeling had come from.

Be logical, he thought. She didn't have any friends or family in Laurel Valley, and it certainly hadn't been male laughter he'd heard. Then the door opened and the puzzle pieces fell into place.

"Mac," Colt said, arching a brow. "Fancy seeing you here."

She'd changed out of her work clothes and she looked freshly scrubbed. Her hair was still damp from her shower but pulled up in a tight bun on top of her head.

"Does your mom know you go out in public in your pajamas?" he asked, looking at the plaid pajama pants and tank top she wore.

"No," she said, scowling. "And you're not going to tell her. Besides, I'm not out in public. I'm at a private residence. Who's going to see me?"

"Your mom when you walk through the door to go home." She opened the door wider and he stepped inside. And then he whispered, "I heard you've been a busy bee today. I just got a visit from my mother."

"Hmm," Mac said, her cheeks coloring, and then she straightened her shoulders and tilted her chin in a way that reminded him so much of his Aunt Simone he almost laughed out loud. "I just reported the truth as I witnessed it. Besides, lots of people saw what happened to Zoe. When I went over to The Lampstand it was all anyone was talking about."

"I'm sure," he said. "And then you decided to stop by and check on her. You're like the Good Samaritan. Your mother will be so proud."

"Hey, I wanted to make sure she was okay," Mac said.

"What are the two of you whispering about?" Zoe asked from the couch. "You're really bad at it by the way. People were talking about me at The Lampstand?"

"The important thing is you're okay," Mac said, giving Colt a narrowed look. "I came over as soon as I could after work to check on her. Aren't you supposed to stay awake when you have a concussion? What if Zoe was here all alone and she went into a coma. I doubt Chewy could call 911."

"I wouldn't put it past him," Colt said. "And because I got a visit from *my* mother, it's only fair that *your* mother knows about your involvement in all this. Gossips never prosper."

"It's cheaters never prosper, you goof," Mac said. "Besides, I'm spending the night at Ginny's anyway. Mom will never find out about the pajamas."

Colt just grinned and ignored Mac's indignant gasp.

"You wouldn't dare," she said.

"Am I missing something?" Zoe asked. "What's wrong with your pajamas?"

"I'm wearing them out in public," Mac said. "If you knew my mother this would make sense. She does not approve of gallivanting about in one's pajamas around town. She's from England.

Very proper. And Colt is trying to blackmail me. But I'm not going to cave."

"Ahh," Zoe said, looking back and forth between the cousins.

"You can volunteer a couple of hours at the clinic," Colt said. "It's only fair after the active afternoon you've had giving the replay of our lives."

"You sound just like my dad," Mac said. "He says just because everyone else is talking doesn't mean I need to jump on the train."

"Your dad is a wise man," Colt said, squeezing Mac's shoulder with affection. "Maybe he should give the same speech to Aunt Simone and my mother."

"But it's like I tell him," Mac said. "We're really doing a service for the community."

Colt groaned after hearing words similar to his mother's, and then he looked at Zoe, deciding she probably thought they were both crazy.

"Hey," he said.

Her face was passive and her thoughts were hidden. But he could sense her wariness. Raven had been right. There was a whole lot of hurt behind the façade of what his mother called a "company" smile.

"I wasn't expecting to see you again," she said.

"I thought you were kidding about the house calls."

"I told you before I left I'd come check on you and bring dinner," he said. "My mom brought over a lasagna."

"Oh, man!" Mac said. "Aunt Anne's lasagna. You're forgiven, and because I'm about to have the best meal ever I don't even care if you tell my mother about the pajamas. Today is the greatest. Chewy gets paroled, and I get lasagna. You're in for a real treat, Zoe."

Colt sighed, realizing that his expectations for the evening had gone off course. He hadn't expected Mac to be third-wheeling his evening. Apparently, the expression on his face let on more than he'd planned because he caught Zoe's smirk.

"Lasagna sounds great," she said.

"I'll fix our plates," Mac said, taking the dish from his hand. "Come on, Chewy. You can help me in the kitchen."

Colt waited until Mac was gone and then moved toward Zoe.

"I'm not going to bite," he said, his mouth quirking when he saw her draw back farther into the cushions.

"I don't know," she said, relaxing and

answering his smile. "For a second there you were looking at me like dinner. I got a little nervous."

"I never bite on a first date. How's your head? Any more nausea?"

"Umm," Zoe said, unsure which thing to address. Embarrassment must have gotten the better of her because her cheeks turned bright pink. "I'm so sorry about that. I don't normally throw up on people when I first meet them."

"I was due for a new pair of shoes anyway," Colt said, noticing the melted ice bag on the table. "You're starting to get some good color on your forehead, but the swelling has gone down some. Keep icing it. And you can take more ibuprofen if you haven't already. Every four hours is fine."

"Good," she said. "The men marching through my skull have been driving me crazy. Everything hurts, and I'm starting to regret buying a condo with all these windows. The sun is not my friend right now.

Colt touched the area around the knot on her forehead, and then he moved her head from side to side gently, testing her mobility. Her eyes fluttered closed and she moaned softly as he stretched a sore muscle in her neck.

He froze at the sound and his breath caught in his lungs. His touch gentled and his thumb rubbed soothingly across her cheek. Her eyes opened and the mossy green orbs stared at him seductively—with yearning—and he watched her breath tremble as she exhaled slowly.

"God, would you look at that view," Mac said, looking out the bank of windows toward the mountains.

The fiery glow of the sun kissed the top of the mountains and cast a palette of colors across the valley—from the palest pink to the darkest orange, and every color in between.

"Just beautiful," Colt said, never taking his gaze away from Zoe's.

"I was totally bummed when you decided not to take this place, Colt," Mac said, their earlier conversation obviously forgotten. Mac never held a grudge.

The spell was broken and Colt took a step back. He needed to catch his breath and get his bearings. He'd never had this kind of reaction to a woman before. He was a man who knew what he wanted. When he was attracted to someone, he made his intentions clear and then the pursuit began. Until it ended. But it had never mattered before, and somehow it mattered with Zoe.

He didn't have steady footing where she was concerned. He wanted to take care of her, coddle her, laugh with her, and make love with her. Not necessarily in that order. And as crazy as it sounded after knowing someone for a handful of hours, he wanted to marry her. His dad had been right—*you'll know when you know.*

Mac brought in a tray that held paper plates heaped with lasagna, along with napkins and plastic forks.

"Why didn't you take this place, Colt?" Mac asked, handing Zoe a plate. And then she handed another to Colt, completely oblivious to the undercurrents in the room. "Dad said you backed out at the last minute."

Colt took a seat in one of the chairs across from Zoe so he wouldn't be tempted to curl up next to her. He'd almost kissed her. What kind of doctor kissed his patient while she was concussed? He shook his head in disbelief. He was losing his mind. That's all there was to it. His father always said the right woman would drive him crazy. And here was the proof, plain and simple.

"It just seemed like a waste," Colt said, shrugging. "I've got the mountain house and my apartment. It didn't seem like good money management to buy a condo when I'm going to spend most of my time at the clinic anyway."

"Our loss is Zoe's gain," Mac said, clucking her tongue.

"Our loss?" Colt asked, arching a brow.

"Well, yeah," she said, digging into her own bowl. "You don't think you could have a swanky place like this and live in solitude. I'd have volunteered to house-sit. And maybe you could do cousin campouts during the summer. You are everyone's favorite cousin and uncle, you know."

Colt laughed. "There's no point in buttering me up now. This is Zoe's place. And everyone knows Jax is everyone's favorite.

"Who is Jax?" Zoe said, obviously trying to keep up.

"My dad's youngest brother," Mac said. "He was a surprise baby, so he's only a few years older than me. Uncle Jax is the fun one. And the one who always gets in trouble." Then she added as an afterthought, "And the one who always gets the rest of us in trouble."

Zoe laughed but Colt could tell it hurt her to do so.

"We need to let Zoe get some rest," Colt told Mac. "Her head is hurting."

"Yeah, you're right," Mac said. "I'm off tomorrow so I can come by and maybe help you unpack some of these boxes. It must be driving you crazy."

"Not really," Zoe said. "When I'm focused on work nothing else really matters. I'll get to it eventually."

Colt and Mac both stopped and stared at her like she was an alien. To O'Haras, it wasn't cleanliness that was next to godliness. It was an organized pantry and a calendar you could set your watch by.

"I take it by your expressions you both disagree," Zoe said, smiling wryly.

"Maybe I'll bring some of the family to help," Mac said. "They all want to meet you, and they'll have you set up in no time. It would be unneighborly if we didn't help you get moved in."

Colt could tell the announcement was a little overwhelming to Zoe.

"Why would your family want to meet me?" she asked.

"Ahh," Mac said, looking at Colt for help.

"You stepped in it now, kiddo," he said. "Might as well come clean."

"Because I might have told them about you," Mac said. "But only because it's obvious Colt likes you. It was my family duty."

"Better stop while you're ahead, kid," Colt said.

"I'm just saying, I think you're pretty amazing. And now that I've gotten to know you better I know you'll fit right in. Since you don't have family of your own around here we're more than happy to play surrogate. So of course they want to meet you. And I've already told you a lot about the O'Haras and shared a lot of embarrassing stories about Colt, so it'll be good for you to put names to faces."

Zoe's expression went from shocked to incredulous.

"Mayday, Mayday," Colt said, making his whistle sound like a bomb that was about to hit the payload.

"I'll take Chewy out for you before I leave," Mac said, calling for the dog and snapping his leash on quickly so she could make her escape.

Zoe's gaze swung to Colt and she frowned. He could tell she was about to say something to shut everyone out. It was obvious she wasn't the type of person who was used to connecting with others or asking for help when she needed it. It made him want to know more about her childhood and the marriage that had left her cynical and disillusioned.

He could have played off Mac's declaration of his interest in her one of two ways—by easing in slow and easy with the whole attraction and going the friendship route, or by letting her know his intentions from the start and damning the torpedoes. He had a feeling she would normally be more open to the second approach. She seemed a straightforward kind of woman who didn't care for hidden meanings or subtleties in life. He would have preferred that too.

But despite the tough exterior, he wasn't sure she was up for straightforward. She had a protective cloak wrapped around her like a second skin, and he felt compassion for the woman she'd been. And admiration for the woman she was trying to be.

"Laurel Valley is a good place," he said. "A safe place. And the people here will love you, because this is the kind of community that takes care of one another. You'll get used to it. I take it you're not used to small-town living?

"No," she said.

He picked up the plates from their dinner and threw them away, keeping the conversation light and easy as he cleaned up and put the lasagna away in the refrigerator.

"Where are you from?"

"New York," she said, warily.

"Ahh, that explains the skepticism," he said, giving her an easygoing grin. "Don't worry. You'll get used to being neighborly. The people of Laurel Valley will scrub the New York right off of you. Besides, you've still got a few days of recovery time. Enjoy letting people take care of you. Your freezer will be full of meals and this place will be unpacked before you know it."

"I don't know how to deal with that," she said.

"What? Kindness and love?" he asked. "Then you'll learn. And before long you'll be doing the same for the next transplant that moves into town. It's the Laurel Valley way."

Colt figured it was a good time to make his exit. He'd figured out his strategy. Maybe if she learned to love Laurel Valley and the people who lived there—his family included—she could learn to love him.

Chapter Seven

ZOE WAS GOING STIR CRAZY. SHE WAS USED TO being on her own and tucked away in solitude when she was writing, but Colt had been right—staring at a computer screen had been torture for the last several days. She'd finally given up trying to get her words written altogether.

She was behind on her deadline, though she wasn't at the point where it was stressing her out yet—at least not too much. But she couldn't lie around any longer and sleep, no matter how much the tiny words on the screen made her head ache.

Every box in her house had been unpacked, her closets organized, and the spices in her drawers alphabetized. She was officially moved in. She could admit that Colt had been right. It had felt good to open her doors to her new community. And even if she hadn't opened them willingly, she had a feeling they would have come anyway. The people of Laurel Valley were like none she'd ever met, and her introverted self was still somewhat shell shocked by the whirlwind of people who'd been in and out of her condo the last few days.

She'd met most of the O'Hara women—she hadn't realized that the woman she'd met at the beauty salon had been Colt's sister-in-law, Raven —along with his Aunt Simone, his sister-in-law Dylan, and his mother Anne.

As far as they were all concerned, Colt hung the moon and stars. Of course, they weren't subtle in their attempts at matchmaking, but Zoe couldn't help but laugh at the childhood stories they'd shared. Colt's brothers had showed up to move her furniture where she'd needed it to go, and women who weren't related to the O'Haras came by with casserole dishes. Apparently, everyone had heard of Chewy's misdeeds and her concussion.

She'd received numerous home remedies for the bruising on her forehead, several new recipes to add to her nonexistent collection, and a handful of readers had come by with books so she could sign them. In New York, it would have made her nervous for readers to show up at her home. There had been the occasional fanatic over the last decade of her career. But for some reason it didn't bother her in Laurel Valley. The people here were so…nice.

She'd been blown away at the hospitality they showed her. Never in her life had she witnessed a community that cared so much for one another—or a family that loved and argued and laughed with the same amount of passion and loyalty to one another. It made the world she'd grown up in seem almost foreign. Was this how most families behaved? Or were they an anomaly?

"Well, Chewy," Zoe said. "What do you think?"

She'd managed to cover most of the bruising on her forehead with makeup, but there was still a slight tinge of green that refused to be covered.

Chewy whined and avoided her gaze.

"Oh, that's nice," she said, putting her hands on her hips. "If you think I look bad now, pal, you haven't seen anything yet. I rarely wear makeup or put on anything other than pajamas, so I hope you keep your expectations low."

Chewy blew the hair out of his eyes and then padded into her closet.

"What? Are you planning to pick out my clothes now?" she asked, watching him in amusement. "Maybe I need all the help I can get."

She and Chewy had come to an arrangement of sorts. She agreed to take him out when he asked and give him treats on the regular, and he promised not to run away again. At least that's what she'd thought the agreement had been. He was a dog with many opinions, considering he'd spent the last six months of his life in the pokey.

Zoe stood in the big walk-in closet and stared at the clothes that were hung neatly. They were too…New York. Laurel Valley was a place of color and texture—all she had to do was look at the sunrises and sunsets to know that.

She grabbed a pair of tight black jeans and Chewy whined again.

"It's what I have," she said. "Geez."

She found a silky tank in the same mossy green as her eyes and held it up for Chewy's inspection. He woofed and his tail wagged.

"Thank you. You've been quite helpful."

She put some product in her hair like the salon owner had showed her, and slipped her feet into black ballet flats. She found a pair of large silver hoops—because short hair seemed to call for big earrings—and she decided probably no one would notice the slight discoloring still showing on her forehead.

Chewy was waiting by the front door for her with his leash in his mouth. He'd been cooped up as much as she had, except for his bathroom trips outside. She bit down on her lip.

"Are dogs welcome everywhere in this town? Do you like to shop?"

Chewy whined and pawed at the door.

"Okay," she said with a sigh. "But you have to be on your best behavior. You already have a reputation around town."

He whined again and she clipped the leash on to his collar.

"Maybe while we're out we can get you a few new things," she told him. "I haven't been a very attentive dog mom. Your own bed and some toys might be nice. And a brand-new collar with your name on it. We're both starting new lives, Chewy. It's important to commemorate it."

He looked at her with the wisdom of a thousand sages and trotted to the elevator.

As soon as they left the lobby Zoe breathed in the fresh mountain air. Getting out of the condo had been the right decision. Even if the streets and sidewalks were full of tourists.

"Come on, Chewy. Look like you know what you're doing. We're locals now."

They waited at the crosswalk for the light to turn, and then they made their way to the center of town. Laurel Valley wasn't a difficult place to navigate. She'd learned if you could find your way to The Lampstand you could find almost anything. Which was maybe the point of a place called The Lampstand.

She was glad she'd brought Chewy. He was so big he cut a nice path through the crowd for her, so she followed along and waved and smiled at the children who watched the dog with wide-eyed fascination.

She knew where she was going before she crossed the picnic area at the center of town. A heavy stream of customers were coming in and out of Raven Layne, and she noticed the suit she'd admired was gone out of the window.

"Sorry, buddy," she said to Chewy. "You're going to have to wait outside. But there's a nice spot in the shade and a hook for your leash. And look, they've got watering spots for dogs all along the sidewalks. I guess this is a dog town. I'll keep an eye on you from inside and if anyone gives you trouble just call for help."

Chewy woofed agreeably and settled himself

in the shade near the watering dish. She hung his leash on the hook provided and stepped inside the boutique.

It smelled of sage and lavender and she could tell immediately that it was a place that sold quality clothing.

"Zoe!" Raven called out, waving from behind the counter. "I'll be right there. Don't go anywhere."

Zoe chuckled and weaved her way through cleverly displayed designer outfits. And then she noticed a beaded curtain that led into a back area that she assumed were changing rooms.

"I'm so glad you came in," Raven said, rushing up and giving her a quick hug. "You're looking much better than you did the other day."

"I must have looked really bad," Zoe said, grinning.

Raven wore a silk modern caftan dress in swirls of color that made her look more like a gypsy than ever. Thick gold hoops were in her ears and gold sandals on her feet.

Zoe had never had close female friends, so she was feeling her way in this relationship, unsure exactly what kinds of things women did together.

"I held the suit back for you," Raven said. "And a few other things I thought you'd like. It didn't seem fair that you were stuck at home and couldn't see what was fresh on the floor."

"Very thoughtful," Zoe said, mouth quirking. "I can already feel my bank account dwindling."

"What's the point of having money if you can't spend it?" Raven asked, waggling her eyebrows. "Though I'd never say something like that in front of my husband. I'm more of the free spirit in our marriage. He can be a little bit uptight."

"It sounds like a family trait," Zoe said, shaking her head. "You should see my spice rack and closet. Everything is color coded and alphabetized."

"And it makes the creative in you die a little inside, right?" Raven asked, laughing. "Don't worry. Not everyone in the family is like that. O'Haras, bless them, and the Irish heritage of descending from bards and poets and lovers of nature, are an exacting lot. Despite Anne charging into your house like a general on a mission, she's the free spirit between her and Mick. She was a Broadway singer you know."

"Really?" Zoe asked intrigued, thinking of Colt's mother. "I had no idea. But I can see it. She has quite a presence."

"She's not normally so militant, but she's been

married to Mick going on forty years, and Mick, bless his heart, is a good old-fashioned stick-in-the-mud. My husband, Wyatt, and Colt and Hank are a chip off the old block. There's not an artistic or poetic bone between them."

"I wouldn't say Colt is a stick-in-the-mud," Zoe said, not sure why she was feeling defensive of a man she'd only known a few days. "He's got a great sense of humor. And he told me he plays the piano. That's creative. Plus he knows how to do a lot of handyman-type stuff for a doctor. He hung all my curtains and put up shelves."

"Hmm," Raven said, giving her a knowing look. "Got his hooks in you, does he?"

"Wha—no, of course not. I'm just observant. It comes with being a writer."

"Uh-huh," Raven said. "Come on to the back. You can spend all your money and I'll pour us each a glass of champagne. And then I'll give you a rundown on everyone you met.

"Oh," Zoe said, surprised, as Raven took her by the hand and led her back through the beaded curtain. And then she said, "Oh," again when she realized she was not in the dressing room area as she'd assumed.

"Like it?" Raven asked, waggling her brows.

"It's Laurel Valley's worst-kept secret. This is the best lingerie shop in the state."

"Wow," Zoe said, recognizing some of the brands from Fifth Avenue in New York.

"Don't worry. We'll get you all set up. Colt won't know what hit him."

"Oh, no," Zoe said. "Colt and I—we aren't— I don't—"

"Relax," Raven said, patting her on the hand. "I didn't mean to make you hyperventilate. There's plenty of time for all that. I have great intuition. Just ask anyone. I'm famous for it in Laurel Valley. But you shouldn't freak out over it."

"I'm freaking out a little," Zoe said. "I have no intention of getting involved with anyone, no matter how strong the attraction. I just got out of a marriage that made me become someone I didn't even recognize. And I almost lost everything because of my own need to be loved. I was desperate and stupid. I can't go through that again."

"Oh, honey," Raven said, pulling her close and giving her a quick hug. "Marriage isn't meant to be hell. You were just married to the wrong guy. Hell follows men like that around and you just got caught in the middle of it. But there are a lot of good men in the world. Colt is one of them. I promise. Now you're smarter and wiser, and you're stronger too. You just need some time to get your sea legs under you, that's all."

Raven pushed her back into a pink velvet chair and then poured two glasses of champagne.

"Now sit back and relax, and don't trouble yourself with loving Colt. There's plenty of time for that. Now is for fashion and feeling good."

"Oh, but I left Chewy outside," Zoe said, biting her lip. "I don't want anything to happen to him."

"I'll have one of the girls bring him back," Raven said. "He seems like a civilized dog."

———

A couple of hours later, Zoe's head was spinning and her wallet was a little lighter. Her head wasn't spinning because of the champagne—she'd only had a sip—but she was starting to think maybe she'd overdone it on her first outing. Though to be fair, Chewy looked as if he'd been through the wringer too.

"You're looking a little pale. Are you feeling okay?" Raven asked, packing up the last of her purchases.

"Just a little headache," Zoe said. "It comes and goes."

"I'll have these delivered to your condo so you don't have to carry them all. You need to get something to eat. You look plumb worn out. Colt will kill me if I let you overdo, and it looks like I already have."

"I can't stay cooped up forever," Zoe said. "It's good for me to be out and get my energy back. But I could definitely use some food and a nap."

"Well, come on then," Raven said. "Let's get you fed and back home before Colt hunts me down."

Raven steered her and Chewy toward the front of the shop.

"Shoot," Raven said. "Speak of the devil."

Zoe's feet stopped working at the sight of Colt walking across the street and straight toward Raven's boutique. No man had any right to look that good in a pair of old jeans and a white T-shirt. Looking at Colt made her wonder what she ever could have seen in Todd. There was no comparison. Colt was a man. Todd had been a pretender.

Colt opened the door of the boutique and

frowned as he looked at Zoe. "You're pale. You've overdone it."

"Fancy seeing you here," Raven said, giving him a quick hug.

"How'd you know where I was?" Zoe asked, eyes narrowing.

Colt's lips twitched in amusement. "One of my patients told me you were over here buying out the store. You should take something for that headache." Then he gave Raven and Chewy a disapproving look. "The two of you should have known better than to keep her out so long."

"You're right," Raven said apologetically. "I just got caught up in the conversation. Somehow the minutes turned into hours, and I didn't even notice. I'm so sorry, Zoe. It's just that it feels like I've known you forever, and it's been a while since I've had anyone who is so easy to talk to."

Colt frowned at that bit of information. Raven had an entire family to talk to. But maybe something was going on between her and Wyatt that he didn't know about and she didn't want to share.

Zoe saw Raven's distress and reached out to her new friend. "I'd do it again in a heartbeat. But next time let's have margaritas instead of champagne."

Chapter Eight

"I HATE TO ADMIT IT," ZOE SAID, "BUT I DON'T really feel up to going to a restaurant."

"I'm not surprised in the least," Colt said, putting his hand at the small of her back to lead her across the street. "You did a great job with the makeup, by the way. I can hardly see any of the bruising. Maybe if you'd picked a different color shirt. Something that wasn't the same color as the bruise."

"Chewy picked out my shirt," she said. "Turns out he has opinions about fashion."

"He also has opinions about lunch," Colt said.

Chewy woofed and pulled the leash toward The Lampstand. There was outdoor seating, and several people had their dogs with them. Colt took the leash from Zoe just in case Chewy was thinking of doing a repeat of the previous week.

"Why don't we head to my place and I can make us lunch there?" Colt said. "I've got more patients to see in an hour, so it'll save some time."

Zoe looked at him curiously and he wondered what she was thinking because color flooded her cheeks.

"You cook?" she asked.

He took that as a yes to his lunch invitation, so he headed toward his clinic.

"Of course," he said. "I'm a thirty-five-year-old man. If I want to eat, I cook. My mother taught all of us our way around a kitchen. She said her job in life was to train up her sons so their wives wouldn't want to send them back to her."

Zoe chuckled at that. "Sounds reasonable to me. I never learned to cook. But truth be told I never wanted to learn. I'm terrified of kitchens."

"Maybe you just need someone to teach you," he said simply.

"I don't know," she said, looking up at him and laughing. "I think it's just that I don't want to learn. I can slap peanut butter on bread or make a bowl of cereal, but anything more complicated than that and I'll order takeout. There's something to be said for convenience when you work weird hours."

"You don't take time to eat when you're working?" he asked.

"When I'm in the middle of a story and things are really flowing I might not look up from the screen for twenty-four hours. I forget to eat and sleep for as long as my brain is functioning in the creative zone."

Colt grunted and said, "That sounds like my brother, Duncan, when he's in the middle of painting. And heaven help the person who interrupts him. The artistic temperament is real it turns out."

Zoe just hmmed and looked at him sideways.

"I take it you know what I'm talking about?" Colt asked.

"Let's just say if you see any artist at work I would recommend turning around and walking away as quickly and quietly as you can. Otherwise it's a health hazard."

"Good thing I'm a doctor, huh?"

He led her around to the back of the clinic and he unlocked the door. She was surprised to see a small elevator next to the stairs that led to the second floor.

"I'm not lazy," he said. "I promise. I had it

installed when my nana was still alive. Nana was my dad's grandmother. I never knew when she was going to drop by for a visit, and I was afraid she'd fall on the stairs. She died just last year. She was a hundred and two. O'Haras are long lived."

"I'm sorry," Zoe said softly. "It sounds like you were close."

"Very," he said. "She was just as active and bullheaded at a hundred and two as she's always been. Her heart just couldn't keep up with the rest of her. She lived a great life, and she got to meet all of her great-grandkids and some of her great-great grandkids."

"I'd say that's pretty special," she said. "Your family is special. I hope you don't take that for granted."

Colt led her up the stairs and let Chewy sniff around his new environment. And then he unlocked the door of his apartment and stepped aside so she could go in first.

"Wow," she said.

"Why the surprise?" he asked.

"You made it sound like you lived in some college apartment above your clinic," she said. "This place is nice. And you have a view almost as good as mine."

He tried to see it through her eyes. He'd

designed it so it would feel as if were part of the mountain—like a comfortable lodge—and he'd wanted it to have a masculine feel. After all, he was building it for himself. The ceiling was vaulted with heavy beams and there was a fireplace made of the river rock that was so prominent in the area. His furniture was brown leather and the rug on the floor a Navajo pattern. The kitchen was almost as large as the living area with commercial appliances and a big island for extra counter space.

"Hank and I renovated it after we finished the clinic," he said. "I'm too old to live in a college dorm and I like my comforts, especially where the kitchen is concerned. Have a seat. I've got some sample packs of some stronger stuff for that headache downstairs. I'll be right back. Make yourself at home."

By the time he got back upstairs she was taking the orange juice out of his refrigerator and pouring herself a glass. "Want any?"

"I'll just drink water," he said, handing her the pills. She looked at him questioningly and he said, "It's just a higher milligram ibuprofen. It won't make you sleepy or anything like that. But it should take the edge off pretty quickly. I can tell you're hurting. Have a seat and relax. I'll make us sandwiches."

Her lips twitched. "I thought you were cooking. Even I can make a sandwich."

"Not like one of my sandwiches," he said. "But I did promise you a cooking lesson. I can swing by your place tonight after my last patient."

"Is it an O'Hara trait to bulldoze their way into any situation?" she asked, taking a seat on the barstool.

"Pretty much," he said. "In a family as big as ours if you don't make your wishes and wants known, and at top volume, you have a tendency to get drowned out."

"Well, in that case you're welcome to come over for dinner," she said. "Chewy and I will happily be your test dummies."

Chewy barked and then jumped up on the couch and made himself at home.

"Should I turn the TV on for him?" Colt asked. "Or maybe get him a magazine?"

"I'm sure he's fine. Chewy is a day sleeper. We've had a lot of activity so he's probably tired."

"I hear you, buddy," Colt said. "Shopping is hard work. I went one time with my mother when she was renovating the barn and it took me a week to recover."

Colt took thin sliced roast beef and fresh bell peppers and onions from the fridge and then got out his frying pan. His movement around the kitchen was easy and familiar, and he loved the aroma as he started to fry the vegetables in olive oil.

"You have a well-stocked fridge," she said. "But I don't see any junk food."

"What kind of doctor would I be if I lived on junk food?" he asked, arching a brow. "In the spring and summer Laurel Valley has a weekly farmer's market. Fresh produce and vegetables. Fresh eggs and homemade bread. You should check it out."

"So it can rot in my fridge?" she asked. "This is why I eat takeout most of the time."

"It's a good thing you met me when you did," he said. "Your cholesterol will thank me later. Restaurant food is filled with salt and preservatives. It's hard to eat out and eat healthy."

"Says the man whose aunt owns the most popular restaurant in town," she retorted.

He grinned and flipped the veggies in the pan with a flick of his wrist. "The Lampstand is farm to table. Everything is fresh. It's the exception to the rule. You're not a vegetarian are you?"

"No, I'm a carnivore," she said.

He added the meat to the pan and then he went to mix up his special sauce and slice the bread.

"Raven said your mom was on Broadway," she said to fill the silence.

"A long time ago," Colt said. "My brothers and I grew up listening to show tunes. Used to drive my dad crazy. We'd be doing chores around the ranch and break into a chorus of *Sweeney Todd*. He always told us if we were going to sing while we worked we could at least have the decency to learn some Creedence Clearwater Revival or Rolling Stones. But somehow the show tunes stuck."

"You've got good memories of your childhood and parents," she said, watching him closely.

The way she said it sounded almost accusatory in tone, but he kept his voice light.

"Great memories," he said. "My parents are a solid unit. It was love at first sight for them and they've never looked back. They put down roots here just like my grandparents and great-grandparents, and they raised us all to believe if we worked hard enough we could accomplish whatever dreams we had. I take it you experienced something of the opposite. Are your parents still alive?"

He got out plates and arranged the bread before adding the sautéed vegetables and meat, and then he spooned the sauce on top.

"As far as I know," she said, accepting the plate and a bottle of water. "I'm not sure they'd tell me if something did happen to one of them. We don't communicate often."

"When was the last time you saw them?"

"I saw my father about six years ago," she said. "We happened to be in London at the same time. I was on a book tour and he was there for business, and we saw each other in the lobby of our hotel. We had no idea we were staying in the same place. He was with his mistress, of course, so that was fun."

He felt a pang to his heart for the little girl who'd grown up with parents like that.

"And your mother?"

"Three years ago. The was an article about my marriage in the *New York Times* and it gave her a bit of status, so she called me up and we had tea at The Ritz. She'd called the newspaper ahead of time so there were reporters taking photos during our visit. It was a very short visit, and I got stuck with the check."

"They sound like lovely people," Colt said dryly.

She laughed, much to his surprise. "Lovely they are not. Selfish and self-absorbed, yes. They care about money and status and what makes them feel good. Which is why they've kept the sham of their marriage all these years, but have always had various lovers."

"Writing was how you escaped?" he asked, knowing intuitively that it was true.

"Always," she said, finishing half of her sandwich. "Even as a young child I was writing stories about a prince who'd come rescue the poor orphan girl and then they'd live happily ever after. I went to an all-girls boarding school with very fierce nuns, so you can imagine how well those stories went over."

He chuckled, easily imagining her with ink-stained fingers clutching a diary, while using that sharp wit of hers on a bunch of nuns.

"I'm sure you were a delightful student," he said.

"Not in the slightest," she said, the sadness on her face replaced with the first real smile he'd seen. "I was a terrible student. I hated school. But I love learning. I don't even know if that makes sense. But I think it's what makes me such a good writer. I can research for days. I love history and I love learning about people and studying different crafts. I just didn't like learning the things that seemed unessential—like calculus and chemistry. I have yet to use either on trips to the grocery store or while investing in my retirement account."

"So did you successfully keep your stories from the nuns?" Colt asked, watching as Chewy unfolded himself from the couch and padded over to them now that the food was done. He was tall enough to reach the top of the island and he laid his head inches from Zoe's plate and the second half of her sandwich.

"Not at all," she said. "I spent a lot of time in detention. But then I went off to college and tasted my first freedom from my parents and the nuns, and I got to write whatever stories I wanted without consequence."

"Did you study creative writing or literature?"

"God, no," she said, giving in and handing Chewy the rest of the sandwich. He took it delicately and then wolfed it down in one bite. "Chewy, we've talked about this. You have to chew your food. You'll get a stomachache again."

Chewy whined and then licked a stray bell pepper that had gotten caught in his beard so it disappeared into his mouth. And then he went and lay back on the couch.

"I was an art major," Zoe said.

"What?" Colt laughed and said, "Are you serious?"

"You have to remember that college was an escape for me, and I hated a normal classroom environment. So I chose a major where I'd have the most freedom and the most creative fun, and I drew and painted and then I'd go back to my dorm and write until the early hours of the morning. My college years were some of the best of my life, plus my parents paid for it because it was an Ivy League school and it made them look good to tell their friends their daughter went to Harvard."

Colt choked on his water and coughed until he saw little black spots in his eyes. "You went to Harvard?" he finally gasped out.

"Yeah, but I didn't graduate," she said.

"Just getting in is impressive," he said.

"Yeah, well I started submitting my books my junior year and I ended up with an agent in one of the top firms in New York. I was just about to start my senior year when I signed a three-book deal for enough money to buy an apartment in Manhattan. So I withdrew from my classes and didn't look back. I sent my parents an email about my success but they didn't bother to reply. Not until two years later when the movie came out for the book I'd sold."

"I hope you're not offended," Colt said, his hand tightening around his bottle of water. "But I don't think I like your parents all that much."

"I've had years to get over it and a lot of therapy," she said. "They are who they are. And maybe I wouldn't be who I am if they hadn't been the way they are."

"I guess that's one way to look at it," he said. "Just a small detour in the path can change our entire destiny. So for whatever you've been through to get you here to this place, I'm grateful."

Her cheeks colored with embarrassment, and he noticed not for the first time she didn't know what to do when people complimented her. If it was about her work, she had a smile and a patent answer. But anything else a look came on her face as if she wasn't entirely sure she believed the one who gave her the compliment.

She cleared her throat and went to take another bite of her sandwich, and her cell phone buzzed. Her expression changed in an instant. Gone was the woman who was fierce of wit and gentle of spirit, who was a little shy and unsure of herself outside of her comfort zone. And in her place was a woman filled with nervous tension and anxiety, and an undercurrent of anger.

"Chewy and I should get going," she said. "I know you've got to get back to work."

He wasn't going to let her off the hook that easy. "Do me a favor would you? I've got to change into some clean scrubs. Can you put everything in the dishwasher for me?"

He didn't give her a chance to respond but headed off to his bedroom to change clothes. When he came back a few minutes later she was closing the dishwasher and Chewy was standing by the door with his leash.

"Thanks," he said. "I'm running a few minutes behind."

"Do I want to know why you needed fresh scrubs?" she asked.

"Probably not," he said, grinning. "Which is why I changed into the extra jeans and t-shirt I keep in the office before I walked over to see you. But let's just say that Dale Beamis isn't having to worry about that boil anymore."

"You're right," she said, grimacing. "I didn't want to know."

Colt walked them down the stairs and opened up the back door. He'd lock it behind them after they left since he kept extra medication in the back room and Doc Wallis had a break-in several years before of kids looking for drugs.

"My last patient is at five," he told her. "I'll stop by and get groceries and then head to your place. It'll probably be around six by the time I get there."

She looked at him hesitantly and he wondered if she was rethinking their date. Before he could think better of it, he leaned in and kissed her gently on the lips. He let it linger, enjoying her gasp of surprise and then the slightest pressure as she kissed him back.

He pulled back slowly, pleased to see she was slightly off balance. "I'll see you tonight." And then he looked down at Chewy. "Make sure she gets home safe."

Chapter Nine

ZOE STOOD IN THE SHOWER AND LET THE HOT water beat down on her head. She wasn't sure how long she'd been in there, but it had given her the chance to replay her conversation with Colt that afternoon and the kiss that had followed.

If she was being honest, she'd replayed the kiss more than once.

She wasn't sure she could handle a handsome doctor cooking for her and making her laugh, and then kissing the daylights out of her. The parallels to Todd were too similar. He didn't cook for her, but he'd taken her to expensive restaurants and the theater, whisked her away to Paris for the weekend. She'd been dazzled by the attention. No one had ever made her the center of their universe before, and she'd been intoxicated by it.

She'd been a fool with Todd. She'd never let herself be one again.

The hot water had done wonders for her headache and the stiffness at the back of the neck, and she felt like she had somewhat of a game plan where Colt was concerned. She needed to focus. She had a book to write, and she didn't need a small-town doctor romancing her with home-cooked dinners and enticing her with the family she'd never had and wasn't sure she wanted.

She got out of the shower and jumped a little at the sight of Chewy, sunning himself on the bathroom rug. He looked up at her lazily and then stretched so his belly was faceup.

"I'm not sure I how I feel about you watching me shower," she said.

He yawned and then lolled his head to the side, making her chuckle. "Not much to look at, huh," she said. "I've always been too skinny for my own good. Used to drive Todd crazy. He wanted me to get implants and one of those butt injections like the Kardashians got so I'd fill out my clothes a little better. I'm glad I came to my senses and told him no. Todd was an ass."

Chewy barked in agreement, and she felt satisfied to have someone in her corner.

She slathered on moisturizer and put all the

products in her hair the stylist had showed her, and then she blow-dried it. The convenience and ease of short hair was amazing, but she wasn't entirely sure she loved it. It had been easy to hide behind her long hair. Short hair left her exposed —her expressions and her feelings. Short hair made her feel like the whole world was watching and she had to be on guard.

"He's going to be here soon," she said. "Do I invite him in or tell him to go? I'm not sure what to do."

Zoe looked at the neatly wrapped boxes of clothes that Raven had messengered over. She had clothes for nights out on the town, loungewear for work, casual wear for the days, and enough lingerie to make the nuns at St. Mary's blush. Raven had a way of talking a person into things they wouldn't normally do. She'd have to remember that next time she went shopping.

But this wasn't a date. At least, she didn't think so. Just because he kissed her didn't mean things were moving to the next level. Just the thought of it made her chest get tight with anxiety.

"Colt is not Todd," she said, looking at Chewy and then back at the bags of clothes. "But I've been wrong before. Just because his family is nice and vouches for him doesn't mean he actually is."

She ignored the new clothes on her bed and went into her closet and pulled out a pair of old black leggings. She grabbed an oversized Harvard sweatshirt that had a hole in the hem, and then went back to the boxes on the bed and untied the ribbon on the smallest box.

A compromise was in order. Her fingers traced over the icy-blue lace of the bra and panty set and she removed it from the tissue paper. It would be her secret, and Colt would have no idea what was hidden beneath the old comfortable clothes.

"It's just a normal night at home," she said. "And he's just a friend stopping by for dinner. People do that all the time. No big deal."

Chewy rolled to his feet and gave her a disbelieving look as he listened to her speech.

"I feel a lot of judgment coming from you," she said. "Maybe you should dial that back some considering I caught you drinking from the toilet this morning."

He sneezed and then padded off into the living room with his head held high.

"Oh, great," she said. "Now I've insulted him."

The buzzer rang and she hurried into the living room, wondering why she was feeling as nervous as a teenager on her first date.

"Sorry, Chewy," she told him as she headed toward the door. "There was no need to call your manners into question. I'm just nervous. I'll get over it. I do not have the time or the energy for Colt O'Hara. I do not want another man in my life. I do not want him to kiss me again."

She'd almost convinced herself by the time she opened the door.

"Were you talking to yourself?" Colt asked.

"To Chewy," she said. "He's quite the conversationalist."

Colt's arms were full of bags and he traversed his way around furniture and toward the kitchen with the ease of someone who was comfortable in the space. She guessed he probably was comfortable. There had only been a day when he hadn't stopped by to check on her or hang things on her walls.

She followed him into the kitchen and gave a sigh. He was wearing an old pair of sweatpants with the knees torn out and a thin T-shirt that had seen better days but clung to his broad shoulders and the muscles across his chest. It was like he knew what she was going to do even before she did. He was not a man to be underestimated.

"You look comfy," he said, eyeing her up and down like he could see the underwear she wore beneath. "I'm sorry I'm a little late. I had to shower after my last appointment. Don't ask because I promise you really don't want to know this time. And then I went to the market over on Main Street, but it's right next to the Pet Palace."

"Mmm," she said, watching the way his muscles stretched beneath his shirt as he unloaded the bags. She was getting overheated. Or maybe it was hot flashes. Maybe she was in premature menopause. It would certainly explain why she'd felt a little off kilter lately and why her hormones were doing the tango. She hadn't thought of a man, wanted a man, or touched a man since she'd kicked Todd out of her apartment. And now all she could think about was Colt and that ridiculous kiss.

Chewy came up behind her and butted her in the back of the thigh to get her moving. She'd completely missed whatever Colt had been saying because the blood was rushing to her ears.

"I hope you don't mind," he said.

Chewy bumped her again and she gave him an exasperated look.

"Mind what?" she asked.

Chewy blew out a sigh and Colt laughed. "Didn't you hear anything I just said? My mom mentioned that Chewy didn't have a dog bed and that you were using your good bowls for his food and water. So I picked up a few things for him at the store."

She felt her heart roll over in her chest. Colt was trickier than she'd given him credit for, trying to win her affection through her dog.

"Don't be a fool," she whispered under her breath.

"What was that?" Colt asked.

"I said that was nice of you. Say thank you, Chewy."

Chewy woofed and stood up so his paws were on the island and he could see all the goods.

"Chewy, it's not nice to put your paws on the table," Colt said, rubbing the top of the dog's head. "Maybe your mom can get all your stuff set up, and I'll get washed up so I can start dinner."

Chewy woofed again and put his paws back on the ground, and then he looked expectantly at Zoe.

"I wonder if he's really a man trapped in a dog's body," she said, taking the dog bed and setting it between the fireplace and the window.

"I've had that thought myself," Colt said, washing his hands in the kitchen sink and then wiping down the counter where Chewy's paws had been. "It would certainly explain a lot. I brought steaks, veggies, and potatoes. Something simple for you to start with."

"Oh, what a nice collar," she said, looking at the tag that had been engraved with Chewy's name attached to the bright red collar. "Very posh. You're an uptown dog after all."

She attached it around his neck and gave him a rawhide bone, which he took politely and then immediately went to his bed so he could gnaw it in peace.

"Chewy is very grateful," she said, washing her hands. "And so am I. All this stuff must have cost a fortune. Let me pay you back for it."

"Consider it a housewarming gift," he said, seasoning the two thick steaks that were on the cutting board in front of him.

"I'll make you a deal," she said, eyeing the vegetables and potatoes with unease.

He looked up at her curiously and asked, "What's that?"

"If you don't make me cook, I'll share my favorite brand of wine with you. Besides, it looks like you know exactly what you're doing and that you actually enjoy it."

He chuckled and said, "I guess I do. I'll take you up on the wine. And maybe you could start with something simple like slicing vegetables. Technically, that's not cooking."

She went to the wine fridge and took out a bottle of white. "Don't judge me for not drinking red with a steak. It drives sommeliers at every fancy restaurant I've ever been to crazy."

"Hey, you like what you like and you don't apologize for it," he said. "I can respect that. I'm Irish, so we don't particularly care what alcohol is served with what food. But nothing beats a freshly poured Guinness or three fingers of Jameson's."

"I'm fresh out of both of those," she said.

"I'll keep you stocked for next time," he said.

Colt put a cutting board in front of her and a sharp knife, along with a zucchini and squash.

"You gave me vegetables for lunch too," she said suspiciously.

"Do you have a maximum for the day?" he asked, chuckling. "Vegetables are good for you. They'll make you strong and healthy so you can get big. Trust me. I'm a doctor."

"Why do I have a feeling I'm not the only woman you've said that to?"

He barked out a laugh and then took the glass of wine she handed him, taking a sip. "Very nice," he said. "I can see why it's your favorite. It's dangerous for wine to taste like candy. Good thing I walked here. Just slice the veggies evenly and then we'll season them and stick them in the oven when we put the steaks on. They've already been washed."

She took a sip of her own wine and savored it before setting to work on the vegetables. "So as an observer of people," she said. "You're obviously the studious type. Besides the fact you're a doctor I noticed all the books in your apartment. Very eclectic—both fiction and nonfiction—but you lean toward nonfiction. You like to learn."

"We're always students," he said. "And we're never too old to learn something new."

"Agreed," she said.

"What else did you observe?" he asked.

"You cook like a pro, you play the piano and you probably play golf better than you say you do. You water-ski, rarely take vacations, and you love your family, though you try to set healthy boundaries with them so they're not always up in your business. And according to everyone, you date shallow and insipid women because you're afraid if you don't you'll settle down before you're ready."

"Wow," he said. "That went deep fast."

"Too personal?" she asked, quirking a brow.

"Oh, not at all," he said, waving his hand for her to continue.

"So is it true?"

"Which part?" he asked.

"About the shallow and insipid women."

"Oh, that's true," he said, grinning. "I'm an organized soul at heart. I like a solid plan, and I've always had one. College, medical school, residency, and then owning my own practice. Those things all had to be accomplished before I could think of settling down or starting a family."

"And now?" she asked.

"If you don't slice while you talk we'll never get dinner done," he said.

"You don't have to tell me," she said.

"Sure I do," he said. "Now that I've done those things I'm ready for the next part of my plan."

"So have you inserted yourself into my life because you find me shallow and insipid or because you don't?"

He hid his smile behind the wine glass, but he

knew she could see it in his eyes. "What do you think?"

"I'm not sure I'm comfortable with either answer," she said. "And maybe we shouldn't have this conversation while I have a sharp knife in my hand."

He laughed and then went about wrapping the potatoes in foil. "I'm not sure how I feel about my family telling you all my secrets."

"I can understand that," she said, solemnly. "I should have stopped them."

"Ha," he said. "I'd have liked to see you try. It doesn't really bother me. I know they love me and want what's best for me. And they all think you're what's best for me."

"I don't understand that."

"That a family would love someone so much that they wouldn't think twice about meddling in their business?"

"Yeah," she said. "I guess so."

"That's what families do," he said, shrugging good-naturedly.

"Maybe so," she admitted. "But I don't really have a point of reference. Don't you get tired of it? You've literally got family around every corner. People who have known you since birth and know everything about you. And because of that, they have opinions about your life. Don't you ever feel…smothered?"

"Not at all," he said. "You're the one who mentioned healthy boundaries. My work keeps me busy. And my life after hours is mine to do with as I please. When I want to see my family I show up for Sunday dinners or make a stop into The Lampstand. But for the most part they let me drive the pace. My parents like to send texts just to touch base, and my mother will bring by a home-cooked meal about twice a month so she has an excuse to spend some one-on-one time with me. But I've learned how to find my peace."

She snorted out her skepticism. "If I wrote that book I'd make a fortune."

"A book on personal peace?" he asked. "Probably so. It's something everyone wants but few know how to achieve. Especially people like us."

"What do you mean by that?" she asked.

"You're an achiever. I am too, so I know where you're coming from. Achievers tend to keep achieving because they don't know what peace looks like. When they achieve one thing they immediately look for the next mountain to conquer. But when you stop to be still and let the world go quiet around you—peace will sometimes feel like a chain around your throat."

She swallowed hard, shaken by what he was saying. It was the truth. She'd set her course for freedom and independence, but maybe what she was really looking for was peace.

"So how do you find it?" she asked.

"Well, I can tell you no amount of achievement can find it," he said. "It's being able to stand in the eye of the storm and watch chaos swirl around you, but stay steady and stable in the center. It's finding that place where your soul is satisfied—where there's no hurt or sorrow or the dregs of a past that you hold resentment over. It's when you can release all of those things that you can find true peace."

She laughed, but the sound was bitter to her ears. "I guess I'm not there yet. It's one of the reasons I moved to Laurel Valley. I needed to be able to shut the world out—shut it off—and find the quiet of peace. I wanted to be able to put deadlines and alimony payments, or my parents not calling me on my birthday, to the side and just be able to float out in the middle of the lake without a care or worry in the world."

"It's a nice sentiment," he said.

"But?"

"But avoiding won't bring you the peace

you're looking for. You'll have to confront it head-on at some point."

"I'm getting there," she said. "Therapy helped a lot after my divorce."

"Hey, one thing I've learned in a family as big as mine is that forgiveness is a process. Sometimes you can do it in an instant. And sometimes you have to do it over and over again. You'll eventually get to the point where you can talk about it without getting that look on your face."

"What look?" she asked.

"Like you're thinking about using that knife in your hand." He took the tray of vegetables from her and slid them in the fridge. "It'll take a bit for the potatoes to cook. Why don't we take our wine and Chewy and sit out by the lake? You might as well take advantage of that private entrance since you're paying the HOA fees."

She looked down at her ratty sweatshirt and leggings and knew her mother would be horrified at the thought of her daughter going out in public dressed like she was.

"You're fine," he said, filling up her wine and taking her hand. "Come on, Chewy. Let's check out the lake."

"What about his leash?" she asked as they went out the door.

"He's fine," Colt assured her. "He's a Laurel Valley dog. He knows where he can and can't go. Isn't that right, Chewy."

Chewy looked back at them and then used his paw to hit the elevator button.

"I don't know if I'm comfortable with a dog who has that level of intelligence," she said. "You remember *Planet of the Apes*?"

"I don't think we have to worry about Chewy creating an army of intelligent animals and enslaving humans. He's a lover, not a fighter."

Chewy woofed and trotted onto the elevator.

"He is very sweet," she said. "Sometimes I just wonder if I need to be buying him books to read or turning on educational television programs."

"It probably wouldn't hurt."

He opened the door for her and she breathed in the late afternoon air. The sun was setting behind the mountains and there was a cool breeze dancing across the water.

"Have you been out here yet?" he asked, opening the black iron gate that only the condo residents had access to.

"Not yet," she said. "My doctor told me I have a concussion and to rest and take it easy."

"You should always listen to your doctor," he said. "You're going to want to take your shoes off and roll up your pant legs. The sand around the lakes is natural around here, but it's more mineralized than sand on saltwater beaches. That sand has more seashells in it so it's a different texture. This sand is a little denser and stickier."

"So it's mud?" she asked, gasping as Chewy made a flying leap toward the water and splashed along the shoreline. "Oh, Chewy. Now you'll need a bath."

"I don't think he cares," Colt said laughing. "He's having a good time. He used to do stuff like that with Lawrence. I'm sure he misses it."

They put their shoes by the gate and she rolled up her leggings while he did the same with his sweats.

"And no," he said, "It's not mud. You'll see when you put your feet in it. It's soft and warm and you can make incredible sand castles with it. Better than the beach in my opinion. Come on. I'll start a fire."

"Wait—what?" she asked as he pulled her onto the warm sand and toward the Adirondack chairs near the edge of the lake.

"Did you grow up in New York?" Colt asked, finding a stick and throwing it for Chewy to fetch.

"Connecticut," she said. "But my father worked—works—on Wall Street so we went into the city a lot when I was a kid. And then when I was eleven I was sent to boarding school in Manhattan so I became a city girl pretty quickly."

"So you never went out on the lake and made terrible decisions?"

Her lips twitched and she sat back in the Adirondack chair while he grabbed a few logs from the firewood rack and tossed them in the fire pit.

"I'm afraid not," she said. "That would have been against the rules at St. Mary's, and the nuns were never ones to tolerate rule breaking. Though I did sneak out my junior year and go sailing with William Bratten on his father's new catamaran. His father liked to race and had it custom made. Apparently it was very expensive. But alas, William was not the sailor his father was and he made a nice gash in the hull against some rocks."

Colt winced. "See, you have made terrible choices on the water. Were you in sports at your fancy boarding school?"

"Of course," Zoe said. "The point of boarding school is to become a completely well-rounded young lady of impeccable breeding and reputation. I played lacrosse, tennis—" She looked at him and arched a brow challengingly. "And golf."

"Ahh," he said. "I sense a day on the green coming up soon."

"Perhaps," she said. Then she looked at Chewy and sighed. "He's filthy. And I have a white couch."

"Didn't you pay attention to your walkthrough and all the amenities the condo has to offer?"

"Not at all," she said, watching the orange flames of the fire dance in the pit. "My Realtor sent me pictures and a video. And I bought it sight unseen based solely off the view."

"Well, if you'd paid attention to the video you'd know you not only have private lake access, but also access to the kayaks, canoes, and four-wheelers. And because my brother doesn't want anyone traipsing in water and sand across his very expensive floors, he installed the outdoor showers and drying tubes."

"Then it seems I made a sound financial investment," she said smugly. "Tell me about the O'Haras."

"I thought we were talking about you and the bad decisions of your youth," he said. "You wouldn't be trying to redirect the conversation would you?"

"Are you kidding?" she asked. "I've told you more in the last week than I've told just about anyone. I've told you about my parents and my childhood, that I can't cook and have no desire to, and that I'm going to kick your tail at golf."

"And yet you don't go too deep," he said. "And that's fine. For now. You're like an onion. We'll just peel it back a layer at a time."

"Why would you want to?" she asked.

"Because I'm a planner," he said, taking her hand in his.

"Listen, Colt—"

"It's okay," he said. "I know you're not there yet. I'm a patient man."

"You're also maddeningly insufferable. You cannot possibly be this levelheaded and even tempered all the time."

"I'm afraid so," he said, smiling. "I've been this way since I was sixteen."

"What happened when you were sixteen?" she asked.

"I was out at the lake with Wyatt and Hank, and a group of guys started hassling Wyatt. He was only fourteen at the time and still scrawny with it. But Hank and I had filled out. I guess they thought we were outnumbered because out of nowhere this kid throws a punch at Wyatt and knocks him out cold. And that's all it took to lose control. Things went from zero to sixty in the blink of an eye and fists started flying. Working on a ranch makes you strong, especially against a bunch of punk kids on vacation from California.

"By the time the cops showed up none of them were left standing. Hank and I were fortunate that Sheriff Cole listened to our side of the story, and he saw Wyatt still passed out cold on the ground. But they still brought us home in a squad car, and there wasn't anything the cops could have done to us than was worse than the blistering we got from our parents.

"That whole incident is the reason Wyatt decided to be a cop," he said. "He hated being a victim, and I think it's why he's so passionate about his job. He knows what it feels like, and he'll go to the ends of the earth to hunt down those who prey on the weak."

"So you've never been in a fight again?" she asked. "Or lost your temper? Why? How?"

He chuckled and said, "That's a lot of questions. But I'll tell you, I got scared that day. I've got brothers, so I knew what it was to fight. Up to a certain point. But that was different. The anger that took over me changed me and it scared me. I didn't want to be the kind of man who could lose control like that. Because there was a part of me that liked it. I had plans for a future in medicine even then, and getting arrested for being stupid and having a temper wasn't part of that plan. Does that answer your question?"

"Hmm," she said and narrowed her eyes. "So now you're cool and calculated. A planner, like you said. But let me tell you something, mister. If you've got me penciled in somewhere on that plan of yours it's going to be a big mistake. Because I can promise I'm not always levelheaded and even tempered."

"Oh, I think I've figured that out for myself," he said. "I figure I need that kind of excitement added to my life. Otherwise I'll turn into a potted plant. That's what Mac likes to tell me, but I'm pretty sure she heard it first from Aunt Simone."

She narrowed her eyes at him, wondering how she'd lost the upper hand. Hadn't she just told herself in the shower that she wasn't interested in Colt O'Hara? She couldn't let another man take over her life again.

"And what are you going to do when I tell you I'm not part of your plan?" she asked. "That I don't want or need a man to control my life or take the best parts of myself and crush them to dust."

"I'd tell you again that I'm a patient man," he said. "But I'm also a friend. I'd never try to control you. Or hurt you. And I'd hope one day, if I'm patient enough and steady enough, that you'd trust me."

"I don't have a lot of luck with trust," she said. "I've learned the only person I can trust is myself."

"You remember what I told you about peace?" he asked. "How to find it? Once you forgive those people whose faces keep popping up in your mind whenever you remember the hurt you've lived through, I think you'll find that trust and peace and love will be right there waiting for you."

Zoe felt the tears prick her eyes. Who was this man next to her? He couldn't possibly be real. No one was like he was. And his words were scraping at wounds inside of her she didn't know if she should let bleed. She'd been putting Band-Aids on them for so long she didn't know any other way.

She cleared her throat and looked at him, tamping down the tears and other emotions that had risen to the surface. "So are you going to tell me about the O'Haras or not?"

Chapter Ten

HE DIDN'T TRY TO STEER THE CONVERSATION BACK to deeper topics, but instead he squeezed her hand and smiled, settling back in his chair.

"What do you want to know?" he asked. "I figure you've gotten to know the ins and outs of them pretty well over the last week."

"I like to hear family stories. It gives me book ideas."

Colt prayed he hadn't overplayed his hand. He'd wanted tonight to be special, the start of something new. He'd wanted to kiss her again. It's all he'd been thinking about since he'd done it the first time. But she'd put up a big red stop sign when things had gotten too heavy, and he knew when it was time to change tactics. He'd seen the tears in her eyes, and it made him want to hunt down every person who'd put that kind of pain inside her, starting with her ex-husband.

But what she needed now was a change of pace. He wanted to see her smile again.

"Well, now," he said, adopting an Irish accent and making her grin. "If it's a story ye want, it's a story ye'll get. I'll tell you a tale of the O'Haras of auld."

"Is this a true story?" she asked, the laughter bubbling up inside her.

"Are you calling an Irishman a liar?" he asked, incredulously.

She chuckled and said, "Sorry. Carry on."

He nodded and settled back into the story, remembering how his grandfather had many times told it to him, his lilting voice gruff with pride and nostalgia.

"Me ancestors found themselves adrift and without a home after the Nine Years War. It was a terrible time for our people. Families slaughtered. Many starved. But they fought all the same.

"O'Haras love the fight—always have and always will," he said, looking at his knuckles as he held them up to the firelight. "And there a rebel's heart that beats inside their chests. So when the land was overrun by the British they took up their pitchforks and axes—for they were merely farmers and didn't have sword or armor—and they sliced through flesh and bone of the enemy with what they had.

"But when the dust settled, it was the British who stood the victor. So the Irish buried their dead and scattered to the far corners of the island, hiding amongst the faerie hills and standing stones, praying for the dust to settle.

"Thomas Michael O'Hara had nothing but a shovel, a strong back, and a pocketful of seeds as he staked claim on a parcel of land in County Sligo with his wife and two sons. He'd lost his oldest two in the war. They hadn't a ha'penny to their name, but O'Haras love the magic of what grows in the earth almost as much as they love a fight."

He stopped for a dramatic pause—as all good storytellers do—and took a sip of wine, watching the sticks being eaten up by the fire. Chewy had lost interest in the lake and had come back to lie at their feet.

"So with the sweat of their brow and a labor of love, they tilled the soil and planted their seeds, building a home in view of Lough Gill and Ben Bulben—a lake and a mountain." Colt spread his arm, encompassing their own view of a mountain and a lake. "And there they thrived for generations, farmers of the land and great storytellers of how the name O'Hara survived."

"Seems like you're wasting your talent as a doctor," she said, giving him a lazy smile.

"Ahh, well," he said, grinning sheepishly. "Don't tell my patients that. In my family it's not such an unusual gift. Let's go back inside. The potatoes should almost be done, and the steaks won't take long to cook."

"Maybe over dinner you can tell me about the O'Haras from this century," she said.

He kissed her hand as he brought her to her feet. "Then what would we talk about on our next date?"

———

She was in deep trouble.

Zoe thought back to the whirlwind of emotions during those first days and weeks with Todd. She realized now he'd orchestrated it so expertly that he'd kept her off balance, never giving her a chance to stop and ask questions or recognize the red flags he was waving in her face. It hadn't been a whirlwind of desire or love at first sight—it had been chaos.

But this was different. Colt was wooing her.

She wasn't even sure people still used that word. She never had before. But that's exactly what he was doing. He was wearing her down patiently like water against a rock, and eventually he'd wear her down into a smooth stone. Only she wouldn't realize it until their twentieth wedding anniversary or the birth of their first grandkid.

He was a tricky one. And he was hitting all her buttons.

"Don't kiss me," she said, putting her hands on his chest to stop him. "I need to think."

His lips twitched. "It's good to know my kisses make you lose your head, but okay, I won't kiss you. Not until you're ready. And then you'll have to kiss me. I don't want to overstep."

"Are you making fun of me?" she asked, narrowing her eyes at him.

"Of course not," he said, leading her back toward the gate. "Come on, Chewy. Let's get you washed off."

"What are you doing?"

"I'm about to hose off Chewy so we can eat dinner. I'm starving. It's been a long day."

"You're not going to argue with me about this?"

"About what?" he asked.

She growled low in her throat and Chewy and

Colt looked at her with identical surprised expressions. "About me not being ready for a relationship."

"Why would I argue with you?" he asked. "I think you'd be the one to know when you're ready. And when you are, I'll be here."

"And what if I'm never ready?" she asked, her fists on her hips.

"Then I guess we'll just have a lot of home-cooked meals, walks around the lake, and the occasional trip to the golf course. And maybe you could come on Sundays for lunch with my family. They really like you."

"That sounds a whole lot like a relationship to me," she said.

"There are all kinds of relationships," Colt said, maneuvering Chewy into the drying tube. "Good Lord, how much does this dog weigh?"

"A lot," she said, fighting a smile as the drying tube turned on and Chewy's abundant fur started flying in all directions. "What do you mean, there are all kinds of relationships?"

"Well, I know the kind of relationship I want with you," he said. "I want the happily ever after until death do us part kind of relationship."

"You're crazy," she said, shaking her head. "We just met. And I just got divorced."

"That's a good thing," he said. "You being married would definitely hinder my plans. While you're figuring all this stuff out I figure I can be a good friend, and eventually you won't be able to resist me. I did like that kiss this afternoon. I was hoping we could do some more of that, but I'll leave that to you. But I should warn you, I'm told I'm very charming. I'm also Irish, which means I have a head as hard as a rock."

"I thought the Irish were drunks and wanderers," she said, skeptically.

"Some are," he said. Chewy hopped out of the dryer and shook himself. He looked like a giant dandelion puff. "But the Irish are also poets and believers of things that can't always be explained. Like love at first sight."

She snorted and rolled her eyes. "Lord, you're a head case. Maybe you need to see a doctor."

"We can play doctor once you decide to kiss me again," he said, cheekily. "But for now, I need red meat and potatoes. And over dinner we can discuss all the things we're going to do together that aren't considered a date."

"You're impossible," she said, throwing up her hands and heading back inside.

"I haven't even gotten started."

Chapter Eleven

THERE WAS A RHYTHM TO LAUREL VALLEY. AND as the last dregs of summer held on as tightly as the leaves clinging to the trees, Zoe found she'd become an integral part of the local fabric. The only problem was she was now expected to join the O'Haras in their massive Sunday lunches after church.

She'd been using her deadline as an excuse not to come for weeks. But now that she'd made her deadline and the book was turned in she couldn't think of another reason not to be there. Though she was thinking of starting another project just so she could avoid the experience. A room full of O'Haras all at one time was intimidating to say the least. Especially since in a small group or on an individual basis they weren't at all subtle about their probing into her and Colt's relationship.

She shuffled into the kitchen to start the coffee and did her stretches as the sun turned the sky a pinkish hue. She put on a pair of old sweats since the mornings had become chilly and put on her old sneakers. And then she blew out a sigh at the challenge that lay snoring before her.

"Get up, Chewy," she said, lifting the side of his bed to wake him up.

He growled in response just like he did every morning. It turned out Chewy was not a morning person.

"Lord, you're heavy," she said, panting. "Do we have to do this every morning? Get. Up."

He growled once more, but rolled out of his bed like a limp mop and then padded toward the door.

She'd learned a leash was necessary for their morning walks around the lake. The first morning they'd ridden down in the elevator together and as soon as she'd gotten on the trail Chewy had high-tailed it back to the condo, ridden the elevator back up to the top floor, and had been asleep on the doormat when she'd gotten back home.

Then the second morning she thought he was going to ram her into another lamppost because his hurry to get done with their walk and back to sleep turned her leisurely walk into an all-out sprint.

But by the third morning they'd found a compromise. She promised him if he'd get out of bed and get his morning exercise that she'd give him half her bagel when they returned. So far the deal had worked.

And somehow Colt had ended up becoming a part of their morning routine. She hadn't really given it much thought as to how he'd gotten his fine physique, but he started his mornings by running three miles around the lake. Then he went to the gym and worked out before he showered and got ready for his first patients of the day.

Since she would only run if someone was chasing her, Colt would lap her a couple of times and then walk the rest of the way back to the condo with them. He'd pat Chewy on the head, give her a brotherly squeeze on the shoulder, and then head off to start his day.

He was driving her crazy.

And it was no fault of his own. He'd done exactly what he said he was going to do. He was just…there. He'd slowly worked his way into her life as if he'd always been there, and now she couldn't think of a time when he hadn't been.

They texted throughout the day. Had dinner together most nights, either out at a restaurant or at home. It was comfortable. And she was more confused than ever.

He'd been true to his word. He hadn't tried to kiss her again. And it was driving her crazy because the more she was with him, the more she thought about the single kiss they'd shared. Every once in a while he'd give her a look and she'd think, oh boy, here it comes, and then he'd go back to whatever he was doing as if there was nothing between them.

She was strung as tight as a guitar string, and even one touch would be enough to make her snap. The more time she spent with him, the more confused she was. They talked about every-thing—almost everything. He'd never asked her about her ex-husband and she hadn't volunteered the information.

It was the elephant in the room because they knew so much about each other it was glaringly obvious they were avoiding the conversation. But she knew he was waiting for her to bring it up. For her to trust him enough to talk about the humilia-tion of her marriage.

She felt like a fraud. And she was still waiting for Colt to show a different side of himself. But so far, he was exactly the person he'd said he was—who his family said he was. He was just a nice guy. He wasn't exciting or flashy, always looking for ways to impress her with money or status. He loved his family. Cared for his patients. And took care of the people in the community.

He was just…a nice guy. Solid and stable and steady.

She'd really only had experience with two men in her life—her father and her husband. Her father was an intimidating man who didn't care who he steamrolled or destroyed to make his next million. He expected everyone to serve him, schmooze him, or get out of his way. He didn't care about people, and he certainly had never cared about his family. A father's love was something she'd never known.

And then Todd…she sighed, snapping Chewy's leash to his collar and heading out for their morning walk. Todd was just a con man, plain and simple. And he'd taken up too much of her time and thoughts since he'd jogged into her life. The funny thing was, if she would have introduced her father to Todd, he would have known right away the kind of man he was. Her father had a sixth sense about those who were trying to run schemes on people who had money.

Her therapist had helped her work out and recognize the issues with her parents. And she felt she was at a place where she'd healed and moved on from those people and that life. She didn't know them any more than they knew her. They were strangers, and neither of them were obligated to her just because they shared blood. And she was okay with that.

But the closer she and Colt became, the more entwined their lives and relationship, and the more she realized she was starting to love him, the more she realized that there were one too many men in her life. She was still carrying the memory of Todd around like a punishment. And he was still manipulating her, bombarding her thoughts and staying connected with her. As if he knew he could still inflict torture on her. Maybe that had been his plan all along. He just hated her so much he'd tried to take everything from her, but he wanted her to suffer for the rest of her life as well.

His texts had become more frequent, along with his requests for money or advance payments on his alimony. Somehow he knew she was living in Laurel Valley, and he'd even hinted that he might come for a visit. It was too overwhelming to think about. But she knew continuing to ignore it wasn't going to solve the problem.

"Heavy thoughts," Colt said, slowing his run to a walk so he could keep pace with her. "I could see the frown on your face from a mile off. Book problems?"

"No," she said, trying to tamp down the thoughts of her ex-husband. She gave him a crooked smile instead. "Just preparing myself to be in a room full of your entire family all at once."

"We do it every week," he said. "And we rarely cook friends over an open flame on the first visit."

"Then why does it feel like I'm about to face the inquisition?" she asked.

"Because this is a small town and you're coming to church with my family," he said, winking. "That's as good as a proposal. Just make sure you don't have inappropriate thoughts about me. Reverend Hughes is really good at sensing that stuff and incorporating it into his sermon. And everyone will be watching you anyway, so it'll be obvious."

"You know, I'd actually had a new book idea while I was out this morning, and I was thinking I should stay home and write it down so I don't forget anything."

"Nice try," he said, squeezing her shoulder.

"But everyone is already expecting you to show up. If you don't I wouldn't put it past the whole congregation to show up on your doorstep and have the service there."

She blew out a sigh. She'd been living in Laurel Valley long enough to know he was probably right.

"I don't want people to talk about us," she said. "Me coming to church with you is just going to fuel rumors."

"People are already talking about us," he said, shrugging. "Let's give them something to talk about."

"Easy for you to say," she said. "You're the local golden boy. Mac told me some woman called me a big city trollop. You're ruining my reputation."

"Oh, I wouldn't worry about that," he said, trying to contain a smile. "That's Mrs. Mueller. She's just mad because I used to date her granddaughter."

"Ahh, one of the empty-headed nitwits?"

"Who's now married to one of Hank's foremen. I don't think she's pining too hard for me."

"Sounds like Grandma is," Zoe said, arching a brow.

"What can I say? I'm appealing to women of

all ages."

She came to a stop and put her fists on her hips. Chewy took the opportunity to lie down and rest.

"What are we doing here, Colt?" she asked, her heart beating wildly in her chest. They'd been dancing around each other for a couple of months. And she knew if things continued the way they were going she was going to have to make some decisions.

"We're enjoying the morning together, taking in the beauty that can only be found in this particular place. It's not too complicated. Doesn't have to be."

"I know you think that, but it is complicated," she said, frustration tinging her voice. And she was surprised that her voice broke slightly.

He watched her carefully, and if he touched her she thought she'd break down and cry on the spot. He sighed and said, "I love you, Zoe. I know you don't believe that, and that's okay. For now. There's no pressure from me for anything other than what you're comfortable with. And you definitely shouldn't feel pressure from my family or busybodies around town. You go at the speed you can go. No one is asking for anything more."

"Maybe that's the problem," she said, scrubbing her hands over her face. "There are things I need to tell you."

"I know that," he said evenly. "All I need you to know is that I love you. I know you haven't had a lot of that in your life, and you probably don't even recognize it for what it is. But you will. And at some point all that pent-up desire inside you that has you so confused is going to come to the surface and you're going to kiss the socks off of me. But as you mentioned, I have a reputation in this town and I don't want you to think I'm easy, so if you kiss me I'm going to have to tell people we're officially a couple."

Some of the tightness went out of her chest. He had the ability to put her at ease and calm her fears like no one ever had. Things weren't as they should be, but maybe she could figure out a way to start down that path.

She wasn't sure why she did it, but she took a step forward. And then another step. There was something exhilarating about the wariness in his eyes. And then the awareness as he realized what she was going to do.

"Zoe," he warned.

She took another step forward until their bodies were only a breath apart. And then she tilted her mouth up to his and kissed the underside of his chin. Then his jaw. And the sound of his indrawn breath was like music to her ears. She looked up into his eyes and saw the blaze of desire banked within their dark depths, and she realized what tight control he'd had over himself these last months.

He stayed completely still, letting her be the aggressor as he'd told her he would. He'd said it would have to be her that came to him. So she put her hands on his chest and lifted herself onto her toes, and her mouth met his.

This wasn't a kiss like their last had been—soft and sweet and gentle. This was a kiss that held all the desire and love and friendship that had flared between them, what had started as an ember and flamed into something more.

Her fingers flexed into his hard chest and she whimpered at the feel of his lips against hers. She didn't know how long it lasted, where they were, or if anyone was watching. She just knew it was the two of them, and she'd never felt so whole.

She pulled back, breaking the kiss, and realized they were both breathing hard. She didn't let go of him, afraid her knees would collapse beneath her. He leaned his forehead against hers in a gesture so sweet it almost brought tears to her eyes.

Chapter Twelve

ZOE'S MIND WAS IN COMPLETE CHAOS.

She and Colt hadn't had much conversation since they'd left the church. Her insides were jelly, and her introverted self just wanted to huddle away in her condo and not see another living soul for at least a month. She'd felt like a zoo animal on display, which wasn't all that dissimilar to when she had to go on a book tour and be in large crowds of people. She put on a smile and shook hands and somehow gave intelligible responses to questions, all the while shaking on the inside and wishing she was at home in her pajamas.

She was still in that dazed stupor of not knowing what was coming next, and Chewy must have had the same thought because he rested his head on her shoulder from the back seat as they crested over the hill and onto O'Hara land.

White rail fences lined the road and pastures for as far as the eye could see. There were horses grazing in one pasture and cattle in another. She'd grown up with parents who had influence and she'd taken horseback riding lessons as a child, along with every other kind of lesson that could keep her out of her parents' hair. Her mother had fallen madly in love with the riding instructor until he'd cast her aside for a younger woman, and that had been the end of her time at the stables.

A big white farmhouse sat at the end of the long drive with a big front porch that had black rocking chairs and ferns that hung from the eaves. As they got closer she could see that additions had been made onto the house from the same river stone as so many other places in Laurel Valley.

There was another big red barn with a metal roof close to the house and in the middle of the two was a structure made of glass where there was a pool and hot tub.

"You grew up here?" Zoe asked, watching the dogs chase kids through the yard and around to the back of the house.

"Oh yeah," Colt said. "Pretty amazing, huh? Every kid's dream."

"It's incredible," she said.

"And more work than you can imagine," he said. "My dad and uncle run the ranch together, but all of us kids learned how to do everything from mucking out stalls to bidding on fillies at auction. And of all of us kids only my cousin Levi has the heart to keep the legacy alive for another generation."

"All it takes is one, doesn't it?" she asked.

"That's true," he said. "And Dad and Uncle Tommy were also good about not pressuring us, though I'm sure it had to pain them a bit to see most of us move on with different interests."

"It's a beautiful home," she said. "It looks like a place meant for children and laughter. I bet Christmas is amazing here."

"I can't imagine being anywhere else," he said. "You'll see when the time comes. Though we didn't have all of these things. The pool house is new and the family barn. My mom decided once she started having grandchildren that she wanted to have a place where they'd want to come. And Dad doesn't even make them muck out the stalls."

"I guess grandparent life is different," she said.

"Have you ever thought about having children?" he asked as they parked behind all of the other cars.

The question gave her pause. Maybe for a moment she'd thought about having children with Todd, back when she thought she was in love and could dream of a future with him. But even with stars in her eyes the thought had given her pause. All she knew was how she'd grown up. What kind of parent would she make? It wasn't a great thought.

"Those are heavy thoughts for a simple question," Colt said.

"Maybe not so simple," she said. "I don't know. I don't have any experience with kids."

"That's okay," he said. "I've got lots."

"What's that supposed to mean?" she asked, but he was already out of the car and coming around to open her door.

"Colt!" said a myriad of small voices, followed by dogs barking.

Chewy was unsure of the children and the other dogs so he sat in the car until both had sniffed him out.

"It's okay, Chewy," Colt said. "They're friends. Go have a good time."

Chewy jumped down from the back seat and all the dogs ran off.

"Will he be okay?" Zoe asked worriedly. "I don't know how he interacts with strange dogs."

"He'll be fine," Colt said, bending down to pick up a little girl who couldn't be more than three. "And how's my best girl?"

The little girl giggled and nuzzled her head in his neck, the love there pure and sweet and innocent, and it made Zoe's heart sigh.

"This is Zoe," Colt told the girl. "And Zoe, this is Mary Catherine. She's my brother Duncan's daughter. You've met his wife, Hattie."

The little girl batted big blue eyes at her. "Oh, isn't she sweet," Zoe said. "I do know Hattie. We had lunch once with Raven and Dylan downtown. But I haven't gotten to meet Duncan or Mary Catherine yet."

"Yes, well Duncan doesn't get out much. He likes to think of himself as a recluse, but he always makes it to family dinners. Fortunately he likes food almost as much as he likes to paint."

"I've seen one of his paintings at the Met," she said. "It's a little intimidating to meet him."

"Nah," Colt said. "He's just a guy like everyone else. When he was fifteen and I was thirteen, he was trying to impress a bunch of girls out on the lake on his paddleboard, and Hank and I snuck up in the water behind him and pulled down his swim trunks. Just think about that when you meet him."

Zoe laughed and closed her eyes. "I do not want to think about your brother naked when I meet him. That does not help the situation."

Colt grinned and set Mary Catherine back on her feet so she could run off with the other kids.

"Well, if it makes you feel better Hattie has all your books on the bookshelf at their home, so you're kind of even in a way. Maybe he's just as nervous to meet you as you are to meet him."

"I doubt your brother is a reader of women's fiction novels."

"I wouldn't put it past him," Colt said, leading her toward the red barn. "He's a sensitive brute our Duncan. And a man of mystery."

"We're going to the barn?" she asked. "I should have worn different shoes."

"This isn't an animal barn," Colt told her. "At least not anymore. As the family started getting bigger my mother said she was tired of people traipsing in and out of her house and messing up her kitchen, so she renovated the barn to be a gathering place."

"Ahh," Zoe said, remembering. "Your lone shopping trip with your mother you mentioned."

"It was traumatizing," he said. "If you look across to the other side of the lake you'll see Uncle Tommy and Aunt Simone's place. My dad is the oldest so he got the land where the original homestead was located, and everyone on both sides kind of gravitates over here."

Zoe felt the tightness in her chest as they moved closer to the barn, and she knew there were dozens of people on the other side who all shared the O'Hara name. They were waiting anxiously to meet her because they loved Colt. Because they knew he was bringing the woman he loved home for the first time. And she was afraid she was going to be nothing but a disappointment to all of them.

The closer they got the tighter her chest became, and her steps faltered.

"Hey," Colt said, squeezing her hand. "Are you okay?"

She was having trouble getting oxygen to her lungs and panic started to take over. What was she doing here? She didn't belong in a scene like this —where white picket fences and family dinners were a reality.

"I can't do this," she managed to get out between gasps of air. "I'm sorry."

The look of concern on his face was her undoing and she felt the tears well up in her eyes. She couldn't remember the last time she'd cried. Not since she'd been sent home from boarding school her third year because she'd gotten pneumonia.

"It's okay," he said. And he picked her up in his arms and carried her back to the car.

Things went fuzzy after that. She didn't remember Chewy getting back in the car, or the looks of concerned people as they drove off the way they'd come. All she knew was she needed air and space. She leaned her face against the cool window and let the tears fall, but only because she couldn't get them to stop.

She didn't know how long they'd been driving —she must have fallen asleep—but when the Bronco stopped she didn't recognize where they were. Colt got out of the car and said, "Be right back. Just stay put."

So she did, rubbing the grit from her eyes so she could better see her surroundings. The trees were thicker here, but there was a clearing of open land and she could see a lake, though this lake wasn't the same as the one behind her condo. It was smaller and it would take a little more work to get down to the shore's edge because their elevation was higher.

Then she saw Colt appear from out of the trees and into the clearing with a big red plaid blanket and an ice chest. He spread the blanket out in the sun and then came straight for her.

She rubbed at her face again, sure it was swollen and red from crying. What had come over her? She never cried. And she especially never cried in front of people. She'd spent the last decade dealing with everything from a stalker to irate fans when she'd once killed off a beloved character, but she'd always kept a level head and handled the situation with calm.

Embarrassment flooded her as he opened the door and she said, "I'm so sorry, Colt. I don't know what happened. But you should go back and be with your family. I'll apologize to them tomorrow."

He just scooped her up in his arms again like she weighed no more than Mary Catherine had, and he let Chewy out to run free and explore. He didn't put her down when they got to the blanket.

"Colt, what are you doing? I'm fine now. I promise. Put me down."

"You know," he said easily. "I find that some-times when things get to be too much a simple cure is to come out and soak in God's creation, lie on the grass, and let the sunshine heal your soul. Did you know the sun is one of nature's best medicines?"

"No," she said, her voice husky. It was all she could say. Who was this man who had such deep wells of compassion and understanding? Would he never cease to amaze her?

He laid her down on the blanket and he took off her shoes and set them aside. And then he lay down next to her. He didn't try to fill the silence with conversation. His presence was enough. And he'd been right, the sun soaking into her skin felt life giving. After a while he took her hand, and they watched the clouds roll in lazy patterns across the sky.

"Where are we?" she asked.

"Redemption Road," he said and she could hear the humor in his voice. "My cabin is just back there behind the trees."

"Where'd the name come from?"

"To tell you the truth I don't know," he said. "All the roads that lead to the different plots of family land have names like that. My dad used to say that when we go down those roads less traveled it's sometimes good to have a reminder of where we've been and where we're going. I always remember that whenever I see the sign that leads to this place."

"Your dad is a wise man," she said.

"I'm realizing that more and more the older I get."

The winds had shifted with the seasons and there was a change in the leaves as they began to flutter to the ground, but the afternoon sun was enough to keep her warm.

"I'd never met anyone like Todd before," she said, her voice hoarse. "I'd spent so much time focused on my career and writing and traveling that I was a bit naïve when it came to men. Other than a boyfriend from college that fizzled as soon as I quit school, Todd was the first man I'd met who really caught my attention."

"You must be the most unaware woman on the planet," Colt said. "I've seen men trip over their own feet at the sight of you. You literally walk into a room and the earth stops moving. You have beauty and brains and an incredible sense of humor. Men were probably throwing themselves at you and you just didn't notice."

Zoe turned her head to the side so she could see him. "I think I'd notice a bunch of men throwing themselves at me," she said dryly. "But I appreciate the vote of confidence."

He chuckled and squeezed her hand, and she felt herself relax. She could tell Colt anything. All of her past mistakes, and the future consequences, would be heard without blame or judgment. She could trust him.

"I'd decided giving myself a solid financial foundation was more important than trying to find a husband and start a family," she said. "I guess I was so young when things really started to take off that I figured I had plenty of time for that. I told you before being free from my parents' home was my priority.

"And then the week before my thirtieth birthday I was jogging in Central Park like I always did. You get to know the regulars. Not that we ever spoke or hung out, because New Yorkers like to pretend they're the only ones who exist in whatever world they're living in at the time, but you see familiar faces and give a civilized nod. I don't know what it was about that particular day, but I stopped to stretch by a park bench and I really started to look at what was around me.

"Even at that time I'd already started thinking it was time for a change. I'd visited Laurel Valley for a book signing years ago, and I'd fallen in love with it from the moment I got here. There was nothing that tied me to New York. It was just a familiar place, and I'd bought a great apartment on the Upper West Side in an eclectic building filled with celebrities of various mediums.

"It's when I really stopped to look that afternoon that Todd came into focus. He was... dazzling. He said all the right things and he was so handsome. Apparently he'd done some modeling in his early twenties before he'd become a consultant on Wall Street. I still don't know if there's any truth to any of the stories he told me."

She watched the clouds and felt the weight of relief lift as she continued to speak. She'd never shared her life—the secret places in her heart—with anyone, not even with a girlfriend or her attorney during the divorce. She'd had no one.

"He told me he'd been waiting for me to notice him for weeks, but I never did so he'd just jog past me and look forward to seeing me the next day. And the next. He made me laugh, and he was spontaneous, surprising me with concerts in the park and weekend trips to Paris or the wine country.

"He didn't bother my work schedule and I didn't bother his, but it was those flutters of first love. Endless text messages and phone calls late into the night. He made my head spin. Which was the point, I guess. And I agreed to marry him only a few weeks later.

"It wasn't a big wedding. Neither of us had a close circle of friends or family. So we did everything at the courthouse and then sent out announcements. He moved into my apartment because it was bigger than his and more convenient. Of course, I'd never even seen his place so I couldn't make a comparison. But I didn't really care one way or the other.

"He was good at entangling our lives and finances very quickly. I started thinking something wasn't quite right about a month after the wedding, but I didn't have any experience with con men. I just had this feeling in the pit of my stomach that he wasn't everything he said he was. But I still wanted to believe him. I let the charade go on for months, knowing in my gut he was lying to me.

"So one day I decided to do what I do best. Research. And I started with his work. It's the first and only time I've ever called my father, but he was happy to help because I was talking about what he loves most—money.

"Ironically enough, he'd never even opened my announcement about the marriage, so he didn't recognize Todd's name when I asked him if he'd ever heard of his consulting firm. I just told him Todd said he was an independent broker on Wall Street and he wanted to invest some money for me. A packet was couriered to me from my father's office a couple of hours later with all kinds of information. It turns out Todd had been investigated by the SEC and had gone to prison for a while. He'd also been married twice before, to women who had very nice portfolios that he'd helped himself to.

"I felt so stupid," she said, a familiar hollowness inside her chest as she remembered how devastated she'd been in those first days of understanding she'd married a fraud. "I confronted him, of course." Her laugh was brittle. "I didn't realize how bad things were going to get."

"He targeted you?" Colt asked.

"Oh yeah," she said. "Just like he had his first two wives. He'd recognized me running in the park one day, and I'd been in the paper because my latest book had been chosen for a celebrity book club and I'd sold the movie rights to her production company. I wasn't completely vulnerable because I am my father's daughter in some sense of the word. And early in my career I'd had the foresight to reach out to one of his financial managers to set up LLCs and trusts and different real estate investments under different companies.

"Todd didn't know all that at the time, so that was at least a nice surprise when he tried to take me to court for half of everything I owned, including the books I'd written and all invest-ments. The discovery packet I received was insane. I had to send it to my financial guy to fill out because even I didn't know all the answers to all the questions."

"I guess that's the thing about con men," Colt said. "They do their homework."

"Oh, yeah. I'm not sure I ever had a chance. It turns out he'd even read all my books. He told me when he read them what he saw between the lines was a woman who was lonely, with little self-confidence and abandonment issues. Apparently, I have common themes about a longing for family, no matter what story I'm writing."

"Seems like he could have used skills like that in a law-abiding way," Colt said.

"I guess there's not as much money guaran-teed doing it that way. The divorce proceedings took more than two years. He even tried to get hold of all my future rights of books or movies. It was unbelievable. In a heartbeat, I saw everything I'd worked for go down the drain. All the promises I'd made myself to never have to rely on my parents again or be under their thumb or roof—I thought I was going to lose it all.

"My financial advisor worked for my father's firm, and he fired me as a client. He told me the orders came directly from my father. Apparently Richard Green doesn't want clients or daughters who are going to bring him bad press. And their name was brought up many times in depositions and newspaper articles.

"He might have fired me, but he did a great job of protecting all my assets. The judge eventually ruled that the trusts several of my LLCs were in couldn't be touched. But Todd was still entitled to half of our combined accounts, my retirement funds, and the apartment we'd shared for the few months we were married. By the time it was all said and done and the apartment was sold, he walked away with about twenty million dollars. Not too shabby for a con that lasted less than a year."

"My God," Colt said. "I can't even imagine the emotional turmoil of dealing with that for so long."

"The book I just turned in," she said. "That's the first book I've written since Todd and I were married. It was all just too much. I couldn't think. I couldn't concentrate. I didn't even know who I was anymore. And I was scared to death to start writing again and maybe discover that I could no longer do it. That he'd taken that part of me just like he'd taken my material possessions.

"That day you met me," she said, licking her lips. "I'd just gotten the final divorce papers. After all that time it was finally done. The judge had ruled against him getting half of my work or any future work, but in exchange I have to pay him alimony for five years."

"I'm so sorry, Zoe," he said. "I don't know what to say other than I'm glad you're free of him."

She sighed. "Almost free of him." That was the hardest part. Realizing there would be a tie with Todd for the next five years. How could she move on while they were still connected?

"I think he hates me," she confessed. "He'd had more success with his first two wives, and he wasn't expecting that he'd be denied more of my assets. I've been paying spousal support since I filed for divorce, and every month he runs out of money so he'll text and text and text, asking for an early payment or telling me how I owe him so much more. Apparently, I made his life miserable for the months we were married and I'm terrible at everything—my writing, the clothes I wear, the makeup I don't wear, and the way I make love."

"Don't let him have power over you," Colt said fiercely. "He's a liar."

"Because you have so much experience where I'm concerned with all those things?"

"All but one of them," he said intently. "And there is no doubt in my mind when the time comes that we will fit together like we were made for each other. Because we were."

Her breath caught at the intensity of that promise. She wanted to believe him. And she ached with the desire that had been building inside her since they'd met. Even though her time with Todd had been short, the damage he'd done had been plentiful.

"I've read a couple of your books too," he confessed. "And do you want to know what I saw?"

"You read my books?" she asked, the immediate fear of *why* rearing its ugly head. Todd had read them a research tool so he could con her more thoroughly. Why had Colt read them?

"Writing is a part of who you are," he said. "Why wouldn't I read them? I told you I love you. I love all of you. And I support what you do. You have a tremendous gift. When I read your books I see a woman who has an intimate understanding of people. Someone who is empathetic and compassionate, and someone who understands the heartaches of real people. I see a woman who might not have experience with family, but she understands what family should be and keeps searching for it. And I see a woman who loves and wants to be loved in return. And you craft it all so brilliantly in the stories you tell, while taking the reader on a journey of not just personal under-standing but also a journey of hope for the future."

The tears she'd been holding back started to fall. No one had ever seen the woman inside the work before, and she was blown away, and a little embarrassed by, his assessment.

"I want you to see yourself how I see you. You're amazing. I'm glad you found your way home to Laurel Valley, even though there were a few detours along the way. And I'm really thankful you got a concussion."

She laughed and rubbed her hands over her eyes.

"Yeah," she said, blowing out a sigh. "I guess all things considered, I'm glad too. I needed to tell all of this to you today. I've been holding it inside for a long time, and I know you've been waiting for explanations about my past."

"I know you've been healing," he said softly. "There's not a timeline on that."

"See, that's what I mean," she said. "You're

just this unending well of understanding. How are you not impatient? How can you not demand more from me than I've been able to give?"

He rolled to his side so he was looking directly at her. "Baby," he said. "That's what love is. How are you supposed to learn what it means for a man to love a woman—really love her—if I can't model it? Not every man is like your father and ex-husband."

"I'm starting to see that," she said, rolling to her side to face him. "I needed to tell all of this to you today, before we were bombarded with your family. Because I love you."

———

Colt had thought about what it might feel like the first time Zoe told him she loved him—*if* she told him at all. But nothing had prepared him for the punch to the solar plexus her words had given him.

She loved him.

After listening to her story he knew what a big deal it was for her to trust him and confide in him. There was a lot going on inside of him—the most prevalent being anger. His fighting days were over, but he couldn't promise he would hold back if he ever crossed paths with her ex-husband.

"Are you going to say anything?" she asked nervously, biting her lip.

"I'm not sure words are the right response," he said. And then he leaned in and kissed her with all the pent-up passion and desire he'd been holding on to for these weeks. He'd been going insane with his need for her.

He realized very quickly if he didn't stop things would get out of control. Their breaths and bodies were entangled, and all he could hear was the blood rushing in his ears.

He pulled away from her and rolled over onto his back, his chest heaving as he closed his eyes and willed himself back under control. And then he heard the whimper and his eyes snapped open and he turned to see Zoe curled up on her side, her lips swollen with passion and her face pale.

"Did I do something wrong?" she managed to ask, though she didn't make eye contact.

"Oh, Zoe, no. You did everything very right. But if I didn't stop us we would be very naked right now, and that's not how I want to do this."

Her lashes fluttered open and she glanced up to meet his eyes. "Why did you stop? I want—I've never wanted so bad in my life."

He groaned and closed his eyes. Being patient with Zoe was going to kill him.

"Because I love you and I want to marry you. When you're ready," he said, before the panic could kick in. "And I want to do this the right way. I want you to know I want you for you and nothing you own. I want you to know that I treasure and respect you. And I want you to know that when you're ready, I can be the family you long for."

Her lips trembled and it was everything he could do not to reach out and pull her close again. She finally reached out and took his hand, and he breathed out a sigh of relief. She wasn't completely appalled by the idea of marriage, so that seemed like a good thing.

Chewy came over to sniff them both, and deciding they'd come to their senses he plopped down in the middle of them.

"Maybe we can give it another try with your family before we start talking about marriage."

Chapter Thirteen

AN EASINESS SETTLED OVER THEIR RELATIONSHIP during the following weeks and into the first snow of the season, and there was a joy inside her that Zoe had never experienced. She had a family. And they were a good family.

Colt's parents had built a lasting legacy, and it was obvious all five boys had the same core strength as their father. They loved their mother, the ones who were married loved their wives, and they worked hard and pushed themselves to be more. Though there was something going on with Wyatt and Raven that she hadn't quite put her finger on. There was love there, but there was also a strain on their marriage. But Raven hadn't brought it up in all the time they'd spent together, so she didn't feel like it was right for her to bring it up.

It was her first winter in Laurel Valley, and she'd been told on multiple occasions by multiple people that a wimpy New York winter was nothing compared to what she was about to experience. She had a feeling they might be right because by the first of December, there was more than a foot of snow on the ground and the view from her window had changed from boats on the lake to the ski lifts bringing people to the top of the mountain.

The wind was brutal as it blew through the valley and cut like a knife against her cheeks. She knew the locals laughed at her already wearing her full down coat like one of the tourists in for the season, but she wasn't foolish enough to let pride get in the way and have her catching her death of a cold.

She pulled the green scarf up higher so it covered the bottom half of her face and made her way across the street to The Lampstand. There were skaters on the ice rink making loops and figure eights around the giant Christmas tree at the center. The sight made her smile, along with the shoppers on the sidewalks and the soft fat flakes of white that hadn't stopped for the past week.

She was supposed to meet Colt after his last patient for dinner and the tree lighting. The familiar ritual reminded her of New York, and she found that she did have a fond memory of her old home.

She stamped her feet on the boot rack outside the doors of The Lampstand and then let herself in. The warmth enveloped her immediately, followed closely by the scent of freshly baked bread. She unwound her scarf and then unzipped her jacket.

"I was wondering who was under there," Simone said, chuckling.

Simone was a striking woman in her early sixties. Her hair was still jet black with only the occasional strand of silver woven in. Her Creole heritage was apparent in her mixed features—skin the color of café au lait, cheekbones and nose from a distant Native American ancestor, and the blue eyes of a Frenchman who'd settled in New Orleans and fallen in love with Simone's great-grandmother.

"Girl, what are you going to do come February? You haven't seen cold and snow yet."

"That's what people keep telling me," she said. "I'm sure I'll get adjusted by then. Chewy won't let me do anything else. I've never seen a dog who loves the snow so much. Thank God Hank installed that drying tube. Every time he goes out he rolls around until he looks like a yeti."

"Oh, well, he's built for this kind of weather," Simone said. "Come on back. Raven and Anne are already at the table."

"Am I late? They're never on time."

Simone laughed. "You catch on quick, my girl. Every time they see you they keep expecting to see a ring on that finger. I think their promptness has more to do with that than anything."

Zoe smiled, but felt the nerves flutter in her stomach. She'd expected Colt to propose for weeks. In fact, there'd been a couple of times she was sure he was going to pop the question, but as of yet, he hadn't mentioned marriage again. She didn't *think* he'd changed his mind.

He'd certainly not stopped kissing her. In fact, the kissing was driving her crazy. It was torture. And if he didn't move things along a little quicker she was going to have to take things into her own hands and do the proposing. They'd have the shortest engagement ever because if she didn't get her hands on him soon she couldn't be held responsible for what happened.

"I'll be sorry to disappoint everyone," Zoe said, taking off her gloves so Simone could see her naked finger.

"It's bound to happen sooner or later," Simone said, muttering something under her breath about Colt being as slow as a turnip.

Mac ran up to her and gave her a hug. She was in her waitressing uniform today of a black skirt with black tights and a white button-down top. She not so subtly looked at Zoe's left hand, and Zoe couldn't help but laugh.

"Nothing there," she said. "Sorry."

"Crud," she said. "I just lost ten bucks."

"Y'all are betting on me now?" she asked incredulously.

"We've had a family pot going for the last month. All I know is the winner is going to walk away with some cash."

"You surely didn't just tell her about the bet," Raven said, scolding Mac. "What kind of family is she going to think this is?"

"An enterprising one, apparently," Zoe said. "I hope whoever wins is planning to cut us in. Seems only fair."

"That's a nice thought," Raven said. "But you

don't know Aidan like we know Aidan. He always wins. And he never shares. It's very annoying."

Aidan was older than Colt by two years and younger than Duncan by one. Then Hank was sandwiched in between Colt and Aidan, and Wyatt was eleven months behind Colt. She'd gotten a crash course on the O'Hara family tree and could keep everyone straight in her head for the most part. All she knew was she had a newfound respect for Anne O'Hara. She had five boys who were all a year apart or less, and she somehow managed to keep her sanity and her house from being a pile of rubble.

Zoe hugged Anne and then scooted in next to her in the big round corner booth. Simone sat next to her sister-in-law and then Raven scooted in. A few minutes later Dylan and Hattie walked in, laughing about something and hanging their coats up on the rack at the front of the restaurant. And then they came over to join the group.

She'd gotten to know Colt's sisters-in-law, and it was the first time in her life she'd had women friends. There was a warmth and lightness whenever she was around them. They didn't always share deep or heavy things about their lives, but there was an understanding of support, even in the unspoken.

But since the day by the lake, where she been able to unload her past, things had started to change. She didn't feel alone as she once had. Every day it had become a little bit easier to breathe and it had gotten easier to share part of herself with these women. Laurel Valley had become her healing place. Now if she could only get Todd to leave her alone for good, things would be perfect.

"I've already ordered champagne and lunch for all of us," Simone said. "Since Zoe wanted to get together I figured we're celebrating something."

There were several glances at her empty ring finger and she fought the urge to hide her hands in her lap.

"As a matter of fact I do have news and something to celebrate," she said. "Do we need to be worried about this snow? It hasn't stopped in days."

"Zoe!" Raven said. "You're giving me a heart attack. You have to spill it."

"Champagne first. You guys know I'm serious about the snow, right?" she asked, winking at Raven. "Should I be worried?"

"This is nothing," Anne said. "This kind of snow is what keeps all the tourists coming in.

This is perfect snow for skiing. Wait until January and February hit. You'll see real snow then, along with some ice. Every year I tell Mick we're getting too old to traipse out to the barn in in this stuff to feed animals, but he wouldn't know what to do with himself if we actually retired. He'd finally have to take me on that Mediterranean cruise I've been asking to go on for the last ten years."

Zoe tucked that bit of information in her back pocket. She'd love to be able to send Mick and Anne on a trip like that. She'd learned over the past months that they were selfless people who worked hard and did everything they could to help the family. They deserved a little something in return.

Mac brought the champagne and glasses over to the table and said, "I might be serving y'all today, but I want in on this party."

"So what's going on?" Hattie asked once the champagne was poured.

"Well, there are a couple of things. I haven't told Colt yet because I want it to be a surprise. But I got a call this morning from my agent that another movie deal has been finalized for my last book."

There were cheers and clinking of glasses, and

seeing the genuine joy on their faces at her success filled her with confidence.

"I only tell you that because the money will be enough that I can pay off Todd early. I've already had my attorney draft up the notice and issue him a check for a lump sum payment. I want to be free and clear of him forever."

"Finally!" Mac said. "That's something I can toast to. What a loser that guy is."

Zoe's lips twitched. Ahh, to be that young and naïve again. "I wanted to share it with you first because you're the ones who gave me the idea."

"Yes, but did you tell him to stop texting and calling you?" Simone asked with an arched brow. "Because if he doesn't I know a few men who wouldn't mind trying to convince him the good old-fashioned way."

"As a matter of fact," Zoe said. "He texted this morning to give me a snide congratulations about the movie deal and a comment about how small his alimony payment seems in comparison. I guess he keeps up with all the news where I'm concerned." She rolled her eyes and took a sip of champagne. "But I told him I was blocking his number and that any questions about his alimony should be through our attorneys. I feel so stupid for not thinking of it sooner. I should have cut the cord a long time ago, but he was able to keep me tethered, like a puppet on a string. But now I am finally free of him in every way possible."

"Here, here," Anne said, raising her glass in a toast. "To new beginnings."

Chapter Fourteen

"You look very festive," Zoe told Chewy as she attached his leash to the new Christmas collar she'd gotten him. It had bells so it sounded like Santa's reindeer were coming any time he moved.

He was also wearing a pair of antlers. Anne had been right. Chewy was a dog born for the cold, and his tail was wagging with anticipation.

"We're waiting on Colt to get here," she said. "Hold your horses. Now that you're dressed it's my turn."

She didn't know why she was bothering. There were so many layers on top of her jeans and red sweater no one would even know how long she'd spent agonizing over what to wear. She laced up her white furry snow boots and then got her matching white down parka, red gloves, and red scarf.

"I'm going with a hat," she told Chewy and pulled the red pom-pom hat low over her ears. "They didn't have mommy-and-me antlers at the pet store."

Chewy looked at her skeptically but his tail kept wagging, so she guessed she was forgiven. "And once the tree-lighting ceremony is over Colt is going to take us on a romantic dinner. Don't worry. He said you could come too."

Chewy snorted out a breath and nodded. There was a knock at the door and she hurried to open it. She'd not seen Colt since early that morning, and he must have had a busy day because he had barely had time to text like he usually did.

"You okay?" she asked, leaning in to kiss him hello. She brushed the hair back off his forehead.

"I'm great," he said. "Just been a long week. Sometimes there aren't enough hours in the day."

"We don't have to go out," she said. "We can just stay in tonight."

"Staying in with you is becoming more and more of a temptation that's hard to resist," he said, kissing her again. This time with a little more passion.

She sighed and said, "That's my point."

He laughed and then took the leash and pulled her door closed, making sure it was locked. So much for temptation.

"You know patience is a virtue," he said.

"So is modesty, but I'm willing to sacrifice it for the greater good."

He laughed and said, "Come on. You don't want to miss the lighting ceremony for your first Christmas in Laurel Valley. I promise it's something you'll never forget."

They walked hand in hand toward Main Street, and The Lampstand was the beacon of light as people crowded the streets and waited for the show to begin. All of the other buildings and shops had turned off all their lights, and the ice-skating rink had been cleared so everyone could gather around.

"Come on," he said. "The family has a spot with a great view every year. There's benefits to owning The Lampstand."

"What about Chewy?" she asked.

"He's fine," he said. "We're going upstairs to the upper balcony."

They wove their way through bodies and Colt held open the door of The Lampstand so they could squeeze inside. And then he led her up a set of stairs tucked off to the side. There was already a crowd of O'Haras gathered. They stood along the railings of the balcony overlooking the center of town, a perfect view of the tree and the shops that would soon be lit.

"Oh, this is amazing," she said, ushering Chewy toward the railing.

Zoe looked up at Colt, happiness bubbling from with her. She'd been in Laurel Valley for less than six months and already she had more beautiful memories than she could remember.

"Thank you for this," she said, leaning up to kiss him softly. "I love you."

He was looking at her as he had so often lately, as if he was searching for something deep inside of her, but she could also see the love he had for her. He truly did love her. His actions had proven it time and time again. He was the right one. And this was the right time. Everything that happened before no longer mattered.

They might as well have been on the balcony alone. She couldn't take her eyes off him, and the chatter behind them died down. And then the lights of The Lampstand turned off completely and they were cast in total darkness along with the rest of the street.

The mayor began speaking over the intercom, but the words were muddled in her ears. Her heart pounded and she had the sudden urge to loose the scarf at her neck. Something had clicked into place. A knowing—an understanding—that though she'd managed to accomplish so much on her own and learn how to be her own person, Colt was a missing piece. When she was with him she was her better self. It didn't diminish who she was or her success. It amplified it.

Music started playing in the background—something cheerful and bright—and the count-down began. She was home. She was finally at home.

At the count of one the entire street lit up with lights and the tree in the middle of town was glorious in its splendor. She cheered with the rest of the onlookers but noticed the people on the balcony behind her had gotten rather quiet.

She turned to look and saw Colt down on one knee, his face shining with good humor and a little nervousness. There was a hush behind them, but the noise from the crowds below was still over-whelming. But it didn't matter. They were in their own world and his words were for her alone.

"Zoe," he said, his voice but a whisper though she could hear him perfectly. "You're it for me. From the moment I saw you I knew you were the one. It's as if a piece of me that I didn't know was missing clicked into place. So would you do me the great honor of being my wife and letting me love you for the rest of our lives?"

Her eyes were so blurred with tears she couldn't see the ring he was holding in the box. It didn't matter. She held out her hand and he came to his feet. "I love you, Colt. I can't wait to marry you." And then she took off her glove so he could put the ring on her finger.

There was a raucous cheer behind them as her new family looked on, and Colt leaned down to kiss her softly.

When she pulled away she put her hands on each side of his cheeks and gazed into his eyes.

"I meant it, you know," she said. "I can't wait to marry you. I'm thinking this weekend should be plenty of time to pull something together. And if you tell me patience is a virtue again I won't be responsible for what happens."

He laughed, pulled her in close and then whispered in her ear, "You want me bad."

"For eternity," she said.

Epilogue

THE FOLLOWING TWO WEEKS HAD BEEN A whirlwind, and she still hadn't wrapped her brain around the fact that she was a married woman.

Somehow the O'Haras had pulled off a miraculous feat and put on a wedding out at the ranch. Raven had worked her connections for a dress and lingerie, and Simone had figured out how to feed and serve more than two hundred people.

Zoe had no idea what food had been served, or even what she'd looked like in her wedding gown. All she knew was that it had been perfect. And after it was all said and done, and the "I Dos" were said and the last glass of champagne had been drunk, Colt had carried her out to a horse-drawn sleigh.

Sparklers were lifted high as they rode off to Redemption Road and the cabin that would be their home away from home. And finally, they'd been able to enjoy and explore each other as husband and wife.

There was nothing that could take the contentment from her heart, even when they'd had to go back to the real world after a week away.

It turned out Colt hadn't been kidding about being a planner. He'd been working double time before he'd proposed, hiring a second doctor at the clinic, and arranging for time off so they could have a proper honeymoon over the Christmas break.

When they'd come back from the cabin they'd started moving his things into the condo, incorporating his touches, especially in the kitchen since he was the one who used it. The snow continued to fall, and Chewy had almost forgiven them for leaving him at the farm the week they stayed at the cabin.

But this was their first day back to work, and it had felt good to kiss Colt goodbye at the door and settle into her latest book. Before she knew it, time had slipped away from her and it was almost noon. She'd told Colt she would meet him at the clinic so they could have lunch together.

She put on her boots and heavy coat over her sweats, and then her knit cap, scarf, and gloves and headed out.

"Let's go," she said, opening the door for Chewy. "I know you're just going to roll around in the snow and make a mess of your fur. I'll leave the leash off today so I don't end up down there with you like last time."

Chewy woofed in agreement and they headed out together. They were almost to the clinic when she saw a familiar figure out of the corner of her eye. It wasn't a facial recognition so much as the way he carried himself. As if he was the only person with the right of way and he expected everyone to watch.

Her heart stuttered in her chest and her palms went damp. But he was in her town now. Surrounded by her people. He couldn't intimidate her here with empty threats.

"Todd," she said, before he could open his mouth. "What a surprise seeing you here."

His looks hadn't changed. He was a handsome man. But she saw a cruelty in him now that she'd not seen the first time they'd met.

"Really?" he asked. "I'd have thought you'd

be expecting me. Unfortunately, you blocked my number before we could finish our conversation."

"I was finished with our conversation," she said. "And I believe I made it clear that any communication was to go through our attorneys."

There were people on the street who were starting to stare, and she saw Raven come out of her shop out of the corner of her eye. She almost smiled. Todd was in the wrong town.

"What fun is that?" he asked. "A little birdy told me the details of your latest deals. I've decided to sue, of course, for more alimony."

"Which you're free to do," she said. "Through our attorneys. That's why we pay them. I'm not sure if you've figured that out yet."

He looked at her oddly and said, "There's something different about you."

"Thank you," she said, smiling. "That's what freedom looks like. Haven't you found another woman to try and con out of her fortune yet? Or has your reputation become too well known?"

He smiled but his lips were razor thin. "I've got time yet," he said. "There's still plenty to get from you."

"Is there?" she asked, her focus shifting to Colt as he came up behind Todd. She smiled when she saw her husband, confusing Todd even more.

Colt leaned in and kissed her as if Todd weren't even there. "I was wondering where you were. You're never late for lunch."

"Uh-huh," she said, grinning. "And I'm sure you didn't get a phone call either telling you I was out here."

"Word travels fast," he said.

"Who's this?" Todd asked, sneering at Colt.

"My husband," she said. "I'm sorry you wasted my money coming all this way to try and taunt me, but it's just not going to work. This might be hard for you to understand, but you don't matter to me. And I'd pay twice as much again just to be rid of you. You are a horrible horrible man. And your days of running cons on women who are vulnerable are coming to an end."

He took a step forward and she heard Colt growl low in his throat, putting her slightly behind him. She arched a brow and looked at him.

"You can't fool me," Todd said. "You're weak. And stupid. You think this guy isn't in it for the money?"

"I'm pretty sure he's in it for the sex," she said deadpan, making Colt snort with laughter.

"I will wring every last penny I'm owed from you," Todd said, "no matter how long it takes, how many attorneys it takes, and how many trips out here it takes for you to remember that I'm still here."

"Is there a problem here, ma'am?" Blaze O'Hara said, coming up beside Todd and looking down at him. He was wearing his uniform and he resembled Simone in coloring, but he had his father's height.

Her lips twitched when he called her ma'am. "Just a nuisance, Sheriff," she said. "Unfortunately this man doesn't know how to take no for an answer, and decided to come out here and see me in person. I guess blocking someone's number isn't as effective as it used to be."

"It sounds like you've made your wishes known," Blaze said, his gaze dark and penetrating, making Todd bristle with resentment. "Maybe you should stop by and get a restraining order. It's always good to dot your i's and cross your t's when you're dealing with fools who won't take a hint."

"Hey," Todd said. "I don't need a two-bit cop getting in my face."

"Is he really this stupid?" Blaze asked, looking at Zoe.

She sighed. "I'm afraid so. He just doesn't realize it. Because he's drawn quite a crowd and I see several people recording this. Which means by tonight it's going to be all over social media and everyone will know what a lying, cheating thief you are. I'm kind of a big deal, you know?"

"Why you little—"

Colt stepped in front of her and took the hand Todd had reached out to grab her. She had no idea what Colt had done, but Todd's face went ashen and an inhuman squeak came out of his mouth.

"Are you feeling all right, sir?" Colt asked, putting his hand on Todd's shoulder.

To all the world it looked like Colt had stepped in to give Todd a helping hand, but Todd continued to make strange sounds and his steps faltered.

"Maybe you need to come to the clinic and get checked out," Colt said affably. "I'm a doctor."

Todd shook his head and sweat had started to bead on his upper lip. "N…no. I'm fine. I was just leaving. I have a plane to catch."

"Why don't I have a deputy escort you back to the airport?" Blaze asked. "I'd hate for you to get sick on the way and no one there to help you."

Todd shook his head, but Blaze powered through. "I insist," Blaze said. "We take care of people here in Laurel Valley."

Todd stumbled away, and Zoe saw a deputy peel off from the crowd and follow him back to his car. Simone, Hattie and Raven stood across the way, watching the whole ordeal with several other people. It had been Raven and Hattie who'd been recording the interaction, but she'd noticed they both put their phones down when Colt stepped in. Not like the video would have shown anything. She still didn't have a clue what Colt had done to him.

Blaze sighed and rested his hand on his weapon out of habit. "I'm glad to say you upgraded this time around," he told her.

"Agreed," she said, squeezing Colt's hand.

"But I'm not kidding about coming by the station and getting a restraining order. A paperwork trail always helps. And it's something you can send to your attorneys along with the text messages. If that guy knows what's good for him he'll leave well enough alone."

"We'll swing by after lunch," Colt told him. "Thanks for the backup."

Blaze snorted. "Are you kidding me? As soon as that guy jaywalked across the street toward Zoe my phone started ringing. In this case the O'Hara gossip network did some good. But don't tell my mother I said that. The woman is incorrigible."

"And determined to find you a wife, I'm told," Colt said, grinning.

Blaze scowled. "Bite your tongue, cousin. See you two at the station later."

Colt took her hand and they walked the rest of the way to the clinic while Chewy bit at the snowflakes that had started falling again from the sky.

"Are you going to tell me what you did to him?" Zoe asked as they made their way up to Colt's old apartment.

"I just wanted to discourage him from visiting again," Colt said. "We're friendly here in Laurel Valley. But not that friendly."

Zoe chuckled. "I've never seen anyone turn quite that color before. I thought he was having a stroke."

"Nah," Colt said, pulling her into his arms. "I'm a doctor. It would make sense that I would know the places to hurt just as well as the places to heal."

"You're like a superhero, choosing to use your powers for good. It was very sexy."

He leaned down to kiss her, and he lifted her

in his arms. "Well, in that case. Why don't we skip lunch today?"

"I was just thinking the same thing." Her heart flipped over in her chest as he kissed her again. "I love you, Colt O'Hara. I'm glad you're mine."

Excerpt from Midnight Clear, the next book in the Laurel Valley Series. Coming December 2024

Hank O'Hara stared out of the window in his father's office, fascinated by the bony branches of the sycamore trees that surrounded his parent's ranch. Twin Peaks jutted from behind the trees— snow covered and majestic—and pregnant gray clouds frothed low and ominous, seeping into the valleys. More snow would come before morning.

It had been a wicked winter, the temperatures below freezing and the wind whipping from down the mountain and into Laurel Valley. Even the die hard skiers were giving the mountains a hard pass this winter. The weather man kept using the word treacherous.

He took a drink of the hot tea he'd made as he passed through the kitchen, and winced when he found it cold. He had no idea how long he'd been standing at the window, thinking of the projects he had piling up or how he'd rather be outdoors than cooped up inside—even with a snowstorm coming.

"You can't hide in here forever, you know," his father said.

Hank turned from the window to see his father grinning at him from behind his massive walnut desk. His feet were propped on the edge as he leaned back in his chair, very much lord of the castle. He was a handsome man—an older version of the five sons he'd sired—with silver hair that had once been black as coal and the blue eyes of the Irish gypsies he was descended from. His body was disciplined and in excellent shape for a man in his early sixties. Ranch life wasn't for the weak.

Mick O'Hara was a man's man and had managed to raise five rambunctious—and some-times mischievous—sons to adulthood, with only a handful of trips to the ER over the years. A success in Hank's opinion.

"You're doing a pretty good job of it," Hank said, tipping his cup to his father. "In fact, if I recall, you usually disappear around this time every year."

"Well, can you blame me?" Mick asked. "I built this house with my own hands. And then I added on more rooms as each of you boys came into the world. And then I added more rooms as your brothers started marrying and adding to the family. I've grown out of my own house. Where else am I supposed to go? Even the animals are tired of me sneaking out to the barn."

Hank chuckled.

"I've got all I need right here." Mick opened the bottom drawer of his desk and pulled out a bottle of expensive Irish whiskey and a box of cigars. "What do you say, my boy? Can I pour you two fingers?"

"I wouldn't say no," Hank said, accepting the short crystal glass. "But if mom smells that cigar smoke I'm not taking the wrap for you."

"Traitor," his father said. But Mick just grinned as he took out a portable fan from his desk and flipped it on before lighting his cigar.

Hank took a seat in the burgundy leather

chair across from the desk and stretched out his long legs.

"You've got work on the mind," Mick said.

"How do you know?" Hank asked.

"Because if you had a woman on the mind your expression would've been different." Mick waggled his eyebrows as he took another puff from the cigar. "I've learned a thing or two in my sixty years."

Hank's mouth quirked in a half-smile, identical to his father's. "I told mom I'd take the week off and spend it with the family since everyone is here."

"A noble thing, family," Mick said. "Nothing fills your heart with pride and makes you want to take up the bottle at the same time. Next time just tell your mother no."

Hank scoffed. "You try telling mom no."

"Did that once," Mick said, remembering fondly. "Still have the scar to prove it. Quite a woman your mother."

"There you go," Hank said, nodding. "It's not that I don't want to be here. It's nice that everyone is under one roof. It's been too long. And it's been a while since I took a vacation."

"That's an understatement," Mick said. "I didn't realize you even knew the word."

"I like staying busy," Hank defended. "And busy is better than the alternative. I've got the new city hall project ready to go, and residential building has increased, even in the off-season. It's a double-edged sword. On the one hand, I really like the money. But on the other…"

"You don't want a population boom in Laurel Valley," his dad finished.

"Yeah," Hank said.

"It was bound to happen sooner or later," Mick said. "People like to build their ski chalets and bunny bungalows. Fortunately, it's short lived. Take their money, son. You know they'll only use their fancy houses a few weeks out of the year. That thin blood does no good up here."

"Good advice," Hank said.

"And maybe while you're home for the holidays you could take a look at the boiler. It's making a weird sound again."

"At least I'm useful for something," Hank said, putting his empty glass down on the desk.

"That's the spirit," Mick said, his laugh big and booming. "You know what you need?"

"I'm sure you'll tell me."

"A wife," Mick said. "Maybe a baby or two. What you're feeling is restless. Work isn't enough to fulfill you anymore. You're almost thirty-five years old."

"And with that," Hank said, coming to his feet. "I'll go look at the boiler. And I won't mention to mom about the cigar."

Mick narrowed his eyes and clamped the cigar between his teeth. "That's just downright nasty. You'd blackmail your own father."

"I think it's extortion," Hank said, laughing at the indignant look on his father's face as he left the office. He wouldn't rat the old man out. But a little fear served him right for trying to meddle in his love life.

As soon as he left the secluded space where his father's office was located, he was bombarded with a cacophony of sounds. Children laughing and screaming as they chased each other at breakneck speeds through the house, his brothers yelling at a football game, and women's laughter coming from the kitchen. And then there was him.

Hank always felt a little bit like the odd man out. He was the middle child, thirteen months younger than Aidan and ten months older than Colt.

A rather raucous shriek came from somewhere overhead and he heard a crash followed by a herd of footsteps running down the stairs.

"Harrison O'Hara," his sister-in-law Dylan yelled from the kitchen. "That better not have been you and your merry band of cousins. If you made a mess you clean it up."

There were grumbles and a bunch of, "Yes, ma'ams," as footsteps could be heard going back up the stairs.

Hank grinned. It was bedlam. Complete bedlam. He loved his family. Really, he did. It's just that there were so many of them. Everywhere he turned, there was another O'Hara in his path for him to trip over.

Hank considered himself a tolerant kind of man. But enough was enough. He hadn't had fifteen minutes to himself in the last week with his nephews and nieces underfoot. He'd exhausted every avenue of entertainment he could possibly think of—sledding, ice skating, taking the kids for ice cream, and they'd played so many video games his eyes were starting to cross. He loved being the "favorite" uncle, but if he didn't get out of this place soon he was going to lose his mind. It seemed like every O'Hara in the house had something to say or argue about. And they all had to do it at top volume.

An excerpt of Dirty Weekend, A J.J. Graves Mystery. Now available at any book retailer!

I picked up the pace as an urgent breeze pushed me from behind. Fresh leaves rustled overhead and gray clouds covered the sun, setting a monochrome filter over Bloody Mary. It was par for the course. Virginia was experiencing one of the wettest springs on record.

I'd left my umbrella at the funeral home, so I hurried my steps down Catherine of Aragon, hoping the towering oaks that lined the streets would give me cover as I made my way downtown. I'd at least had the foresight to put on my black parka as I'd let myself out the back door.

My name is J.J. Graves and there was peace in the monotony of routine. For the last several months I'd decided getting fresh air and exercise might be good for me, so I'd gotten into the habit of arriving at the funeral home early and walking to the Towne Square for my morning coffee. It wasn't a hardship. Jack said I made terrible coffee. My coffee kept me awake and functional, especially during my residency at the hospital, so I'd learned to endure.

The fact that I usually bought a donut to go

with my coffee probably balanced out the calories I worked off on my walk. I'm a stress eater, so I don't really have an excuse. I'm just fortunate I still have my metabolism, but I hear that will disappear by the time I'm forty and all those donuts will catch up to me.

You might be wondering why I'm stress eating. It's an easy enough answer. It's also the same reason I decided that exercise and fresh air might be good for me. Jack and I have been trying to have a baby for the past six months or so. So far, we haven't had any luck, though we've had loads of practice.

I'm a doctor, so I know how these things work. It's too soon to be worried about why I'm not pregnant yet, and there could be any number of sound medical reasons. I tend to lean toward the idea that my stress is caused by my career choices. If the things I've seen in life affect my mind and body in strange ways, I figure my reproductive system has its own kind of PTSD to deal with and it's just trying to figure out what normal is. The rest of me was still trying to figure out what normal was too.

The funeral home was my day job. I was fourth-generation mortician, and Graves Funeral Home was finally running in the black and on the right side of the law. My family would probably be devastated to know this, but they're too busy hauling coal in hell to care too much.

I used to say that being a mortician was in my blood, but since I found out that the family I'd thought were mine were nothing more than frauds, con artists, and criminals—not to mention kidnappers since they'd taken me from my birth mother—I don't feel the familial guilt I once did for not willingly taking over the reins of my inheritance.

Running a funeral home is like most jobs, I imagine. There's a lot of organization and customer service involved. We provide a service of dignity and respect. With the added touch of pumping people's loved ones full of embalming fluid, cremating them in a fiery furnace, or burying them six feet under. It was an irony that didn't go unnoticed.

I'd grown the business to the point where I didn't have to be as hands on as I once had. I was kind of like a death CPA. I had a bunch of interns and staff who did most of the grimy work, and my signature went on everything because the government likes to have someone to blame and tax.

Along with the funeral home, I was also the

coroner for King George County, which occupied most of the other hours of my day. The upside to this was that I got to work alongside Jack. The downside was we lived and breathed the job, and we typically saw the worst humanity had to offer. People were generally good, and we tried to remember that. But when you put them in situations like murder investigations there was a basic instinct that crept from the depths of the soul for self-preservation. We always assume everyone is lying in a murder investigation. It made our jobs easier. It didn't translate so well though when we were off the job.

The least stressful part of either of my jobs was working with the dead. The dead never disappointed, they were always consistent, and they never talked back. It was the living that made things challenging. Plus, there was the stress I put on myself. Like worrying about why I still wasn't pregnant. It was a never-ending cycle of pressure.

I picked up the pace and waved to the driver of a blue sedan as I crossed the intersection and headed toward the Towne Square. I passed newly renovated condos and walked under a scaffold of another historic building that would end up being a homemade soap or boba tea shop. King George County was becoming another Charleston or

Savannah, with its trendy shops and rising real estate costs.

But the citizens of King George were fighters and they didn't give up their land lightly. The area might be growing and new businesses and families moving in, but it wasn't big box corporations and billionaire developers. And it wasn't federal agencies from DC encroaching and trying to take what wasn't theirs. We knew these attempts were happening for a fact because our friend Carver had discovered things he wasn't supposed to know while working for the FBI. Now he was a man on the run and we hadn't heard from him in months.

"Morning, Doc," Officer Cheek said as he headed to his patrol car. He was fresh faced and spit and polished in his uniform for the start of his shift, and he held a to-go cup of coffee and a bag of donuts from Lady Jane's.

"Morning, Cheek," I said, and then I tortured myself as I passed by Lady Jane's and inhaled the most incredible aromas of powdered sugar and fried dough.

I told myself it was the line out the door that had me walking past Lady Jane's, but that was a lie. I would have stood in line for hours to taste those sweet confections and the best coffee on this side of the Atlantic. It was only a deep loyalty and friendship that had me walking past Lady Jane's and continuing across the square to the Donut Palace.

My receptionist, Emmy Lu, had been dating Tom Daly for the good part of a year now. I'd gone to kindergarten with Tom and he was a great guy, but he probably would've had more success opening a butcher shop or a bar. Tom was a guy's guy, and he was as basic as they came. He was meat and potatoes. He was a plain glazed donut. But he was solid and stable, and what he didn't make in donut income he made up for as a handyman.

All these things were important because Emmy Lu loved him, and she had five boys to raise since her no-good ex-husband left her high and dry. But the Donut Palace had been a staple the last twenty-five years, run by Tom's father before he passed, and Emmy Lu worked there for extra money four days a week. I wasn't sure how Tom could afford to pay her, but that probably had more to do with hormones than best business practices. The last thing I wanted was for Tom and Emmy Lu to be in a financial fix, so I passed by Lady Jane's every morning and walked straight to the Donut Palace, where there was no line out the door and plenty of donuts on the shelf.

"Morning," I said, as the little bell tinkled above the door.

"Morning, Jaye," Emmy Lu said from behind the counter. She was a short, plump woman with a kind face and dimples. If I had to think of Suzy Homemaker, Emmy Lu is who'd come to mind. She wore a white apron over a waist that had been thickened by five pregnancies and donuts, and her fluffy brown hair was piled on top of her head in a messy bun.

"I was wondering if you were going to make it in this morning," she said. "It's looking nasty out there."

On the mornings Emmy Lu worked at the Donut Palace, she opened with Tom at four and then she'd stay and work the counter until she had to be at the funeral home at nine. I didn't know where she found the energy to work two jobs and raise five boys, but if I was a betting woman, I'd bet that Emmy Lu could probably rule the world and still make cookies at the end of the day.

"Forecast says there's no end in sight," I said. "We've got two graveside services this weekend, and six-foot holes that are going to be full of muddy water. The last two days were a reprieve. I'm hoping the excavator can get into the cemetery and get those holes dug this morning without getting stuck. I tried to talk the families out of doing a graveside service and using the funeral home instead, but people get ideas in their heads of how they want things to be and there's no convincing them otherwise."

Emmy Lu clicked her tongue in sympathy. "I don't know why people insist on a graveside service when they know good and well the weather here is as fickle as Norma Greenbough's dating life since her husband died."

I grunted in agreement.

"Norma's all over the place," Emmy Lu said. "Signing up for a Tinder account one minute and then after she swipes right she's beating the men off with a stick and telling them she's not interested. No one wants to see a woman her age on Tinder."

I hmmed and let out a quiet sigh of disappointment as I looked into the donut case. There were no bear claws or apple fritters. No cream- or jelly-filled donuts. It was just glazed and chocolate and what looked like a sad blueberry cake donut on the bottom shelf.

"People grieve in different ways," I said.

Emmy Lu snorted and bent over the case to put two chocolate donuts in a bag. "She's not grieving if you ask me. I think she's feeling guilty.

Jimmy Martin is the manager over at Stromboli's and I heard it straight from his lips that Norma was berating Richard up one side and down the other because he forgot their anniversary. Jimmy said Richard looked straight at Norma, told her to shut up, and then fell face-first in his tiramisu. Didn't even get to finish it first before he died."

I grinned and poured coffee from a carafe into an insulated cup and was liberal with the cream and sugar to ease the bitterness.

"The pool of potential male candidates on Tinder in King George can't be many," I said. "Norma will run out of choices eventually. In the meantime, we've got Bruce Lichner and Merilee Walling to bury in a watery grave this weekend. And all their friends and family can stand graveside and be miserable with them."

Emmy Lu shivered. "Fifty dollars says there's twice as many people who show up after the service for the casseroles and dessert bar."

"That's a sucker's bet," I said.

Tom poked his head from around back and said, "Morning, J.J. Just pulling a fresh batch from the ovens. You got here just in time before the rush."

Emmy Lu met my eyes and her brows rose to her hairline, but she didn't say anything. She didn't have to. Everything she was thinking was written right across her face. Emmy Lu was a terrible poker player.

"Take your time coming in this morning," I told her. "The schedule is clear until this afternoon when we have to start prepping for viewings."

Emmy Lu clucked her tongue and said, "If you ask me, digging watery graves is going to be the least of our problems this weekend. It's Friday the thirteenth and a full moon."

I shuddered and said, "I hate full moons. I thought it was bad when I worked at the hospital, but I had some of my most interesting patients show up when there was a full moon. Like the guy who accidentally shot himself in the head with his nail gun."

Emmy Lu snickered and bit into her own donut.

"Drove himself to the hospital and was sitting in the waiting room bold as you please next to a kid who'd broken his arm jumping off his roof and into a swimming pool. But full moons are a whole different animal now that I'm the coroner. Generally full moon bad decisions end with a body bag instead of an nail extraction and a cast."

"Well, good luck," Emmy Lu said. "I'll either see you at the office this afternoon or sometime next week."

I paid and said my goodbyes, having every intention of heading over to the sheriff's office to see if I could bum a Lady Jane's donut from the breakroom, but my phone rang before I could step foot in that direction.

"Graves," I said, recognizing the number from dispatch.

"You've got a body at 1822 Monastery Court in Bloody Mary," Barbara Blanton said. "Sheriff is already on scene and requesting the coroner."

"I'm about ten minutes out," I said and disconnected before I got stuck on the phone with Barbara. If you wanted to know anything about anyone, Barbara was the person to see. Most of the time it was the truth too.

I looked up at the sky again and swore under my breath as a low rumble of thunder vibrated the air around me. I took back my earlier sentiment about there being peace in routine. If I'd had the sense that God gave a goose I'd have taken one look at the sky and driven in my car to get donuts and coffee. That same goose sense probably would have taken me straight to Lady

Jane's instead of clear across the other side of the Towne Square.

"You okay, Doc?" asked a familiar voice.

A patrol car had pulled right in front of me and I'd been so busy condemning my bad decisions that I hadn't even noticed. Officer Chen sat behind the wheel of her black-and-white and the look on her face made me wonder how long she'd been trying to get my attention.

"I'm fine," I said. "Just regretting some life choices."

She looked at the Donut Palace coffee and bag of donuts in my hand and nodded sympathetically. "We've all been there."

"I just got the call for the body pickup on Monastery Court," I said. "My car is at the funeral home."

"Oh," she said, realizing I'd been full of a myriad of bad life choices that morning. "Hop in. I can swing you by. I heard it was a real doozy."

"Homicide?" I asked.

"Don't know the details," she said, shrugging. "But I'd take your boots. I heard it was real messy."

"Lovely," I said.

"You should eat a donut. You're going to need some fortification." She looked at my donut bag again. "Of course, it's times like these you need real sugar. Or maybe a cream-filled."

I sighed dejectedly and said, "You're right." Then I tossed the coffee and donut bag into the nearest trash can before I got in the patrol car.

Liliana Hart is a *New York Times*, *USA Today*, and Publisher's Weekly bestselling author of more than eighty titles. After starting her first novel her freshman year of college, she immediately became addicted to writing and knew she'd found what she was meant to do with her life. She has no idea why she majored in music.

Since publishing in June 2011, Liliana has sold more than ten-million books. All three of her series have made multiple appearances on the New York Times list.

Liliana can almost always be found at her computer writing, hauling five kids to various activities, or spending time with her husband. She calls Texas home.

If you enjoyed reading this book, I would appreciate it if you would help others enjoy this book too.

Recommend it. Please help other readers find this book by recommending it to friends, readers' groups and discussion boards.

Review it. Please tell other readers why you liked this book by reviewing.

Connect with me online:
www.lilianahart.com

Also by Liliana Hart

Laurel Valley

Tribulation Pass

Redemption Road

Midnight Clear

JJ Graves Mystery Series

Dirty Little Secrets

A Dirty Shame

Dirty Rotten Scoundrel

Down and Dirty

Dirty Deeds

Dirty Laundry

Dirty Money

A Dirty Job

Dirty Devil

Playing Dirty

Dirty Martini

Dirty Dozen

Dirty Minds

Dirty Weekend

Dirty Looks

Addison Holmes Mystery Series

Whiskey Rebellion

Whiskey Sour

Whiskey For Breakfast

Whiskey, You're The Devil

Whiskey on the Rocks

Whiskey Tango Foxtrot

Whiskey and Gunpowder

Whiskey Lullaby

The Scarlet Chronicles

Bouncing Betty

Hand Grenade Helen

Front Line Francis

The Harley and Davidson Mystery Series

The Farmer's Slaughter

A Tisket a Casket

I Saw Mommy Killing Santa Claus

Get Your Murder Running

Deceased and Desist

Malice in Wonderland

Tequila Mockingbird

Gone With the Sin

Grime and Punishment

Blazing Rattles

A Salt and Battery

Curl Up and Dye

First Comes Death Then Comes Marriage

Box Set 1

Box Set 2

Box Set 3

The Gravediggers

The Darkest Corner

Gone to Dust

Say No More